T0078418

The Engraved Palm

ANNE COLBERT

WESTBOW
PRESS®
A DIVISION OF THOMAS NELSON
& ZONDERVAN

WestBow Press books may be ordered through booksellers or by contacting:

WestBow Press
A Division of Thomas Nelson & Zondervan
1663 Liberty Drive
Bloomington, IN 47403
www.westbowpress.com
844-714-3454

ISBN: 978-1-6642-1710-2 (sc)
ISBN: 978-1-6642-1709-6 (hc)
ISBN: 978-1-6642-1711-9 (e)

Library of Congress Control Number: 2020925396

Print information available on the last page.

WestBow Press rev. date: 01/06/2020

Accepting that our mental health deserve the same care as the physical part of our bodies is a crucial step toward healing, especially when in an environment of inequity.

To my God and Creator, who has given me His peace, which goes beyond understandings, and guards my heart and mind in Christ Jesus

I serve You always. I give You all the praise and glory for everything I am and everything I have; it is because of You. Thank you for always being with me and helping me since my conception. Without Your help, I would not have made it in this life. There are not enough words to express all I feel in my heart for You. I will worship You until my last breath.

To my mother, Pauline

What strength you had throughout your life in insurmountable circumstances and tragedies. I am grateful I was able to tell you that I realized that fact before God called you home. All you ever wanted was to love and care for your family and live a normal life. Because of your great love for your family, your trust in God, and the help from the physicians and mental health professionals, you were able to experience years of a healed, happy life. You are the example of a victorious woman—spiritually, physically, emotionally, and mentally. I am proud to be your daughter. I love and miss you, but I will see you and will hold you in my arms when I get there, when our Creator calls me home.

To all the beautiful people of color and of mixed heritage

May each of you walk in the same peace I walk in on this journey on earth. Know that you are fearfully and wonderfully made, that God constantly has guard over your heart and mind, and that no person can pluck you out of your Father's hand.

Finally and of most importance, to the immeasurable number of people of all races across the world and their loved ones who are hurting, emotionally and mentally

A Mental Health Condition is much more common than we may think. Because of ignorance and stigmas, those who are suffering the most are those who are in hiding. God sees the suffering of everyone and promises us that He will always be present and will not leave anyone alone. God also promises that He will give us a way of escape—and He will; I have seen it.

There is help and there is happiness. I dedicate this book and my life to all of you. Please don't give up. You have a purpose. Fulfill it.

ACKNOWLEDGMENTS

This book would not have been written without the love and support of my husband, Herman Colbert Jr., and his unfailing love and devotion to me and our beautiful family. I appreciate every action you took physically and spiritually to help create this book. I thank my Creator for our many years together, and I am blessed I get to spend the rest of my life with you.

To my children—Dionadre, Elisa, and Paula: you are beautiful beacons that shine brightly. I am so proud of the adults you have become and the work you all do to help others in this life.

To my grandchildren—Courtney, Rell, De'Leayah, Kaylin, Dionadre, Dakarai, Keeley, Kalyx, and Payton: thank you for the love and motivation you give me. Each of you has wonderful gifts and talents. You are all a great blessing in my life. I look forward to watching all of you continue to grow and to seeing how God will continue to use you in in His work for the kingdom of God.

To my beautiful niece, Rita: without you and your encouragement, I never would have taken that leap of faith and begun to write eighteen years ago. This acknowledgment is long overdue, and I give you all my love, admiration, and appreciation for who you are as a person, a mother, and a wonderful woman of God.

To achieve and live a life of victory, mentally and emotionally, especially amid injustice and trauma, mandates the decision to read or hear God's Word daily. Never minimize the value of one or two scriptures daily; it is vital. Trusting God completely, no matter the circumstance, is the glue that seals our relationships with Him. Utilizing the help that God has made available through reliable mental health professionals with integrity is unlocking your personal treasure chest full of valuables and producing an abundantly rich life.

CHAPTER 1

The Road to Love

M y feet are starting to hurt a little in these shoes today. Usually, they don't hurt so soon when we're walking to my grandparents' house. The ground is still wet from the southern downpour last night. All the gravel is loose and muddy. My feet will love it when we get to Big Ma and Papa's. I will stick my feet in the nice warm pond.

My name is Colleen Spencer. I live in Senoia, Georgia, and it is the summer of 1926. Mama and Auntie are keeping up a swift pace ahead of me, like they always do when we must get back home before sunset. Looking at them from the back is like looking at the same person, both shaped with the same small shoulders, thin waist, and wide hips. They both wear their hair with bangs and a long, curly, thick ponytail that falls past their shoulders and down their backs. Auntie's hair is shiny black, and my mama's is a beautiful chestnut brown, with sandy brown and golden streaks in it.

Auntie is my great-auntie; she is Big Ma's baby sister, but she is just six years older than my mama. Big Ma calls them two sweet peas in one pod. They've done everything together since Mama was born, Papa said. Auntie told me she became a big girl when Mama was born because she always helped Big Ma with Mama. I think they act more like sisters, even if they are aunt and niece.

They both have big, strong legs. Big Ma says my legs will be like that too because I always help her in the garden when I visit. I help with her yard chores too. Ruthie, my younger sister, always walks directly behind Mama and Auntie and in front of me. She thinks she is boss over me, even though I'm two years older. That's okay; she is much braver than me in some circumstances.

This excursion is the highlight of each week for us, going to visit the people I love the most, besides my mama and auntie. I have such a special feeling that warms my heart when I even think of these two people. They are the best of the best, and I am proud to say they are my grandparents. They are the ones who make me feel that I can do anything. When I become a woman, I will have a life just like them and a wonderful home full of love—a safe and untroubled home.

I do not mind the walk—it is worth it, even though it takes a few hours. Our pace always picks up as we get closer. Auntie lives with us, but sometimes she stays with Big Ma and Papa when we go back home. *Papa* is the name we call our grandfather.

If I could stay and never leave them, I would. When you say the word *love*, that's who I see in my mind immediately—my Big Ma and Papa. Ever since I can remember, they have always been there waiting—waiting for us to arrive at their house—with open arms and lots of laughter.

A large brown house with a sprawling wrap-around porch awaits Mama and Auntie, me and Ruthie, and my youngest sister, Opal (but we call her *Baby Girl*). She is four years younger than me.

Oh, my Baby Girl—I must hold her hand right now as we walk. If I didn't have a good hold on her, she would take off running from this dusty road and into an abundance of trees. It's a habit of hers; she likes for me to chase her until she falls and gets scrapes on her knees and hands.

Whenever she recovers from the initial fall, I will have to carry her the rest of the way, or she will cry like it's the end of her world. That is another reason I think I will have big, strong legs—carrying this load of a girl once a week.

We all love to visit at Big Ma and Papa's. My mama, especially, loves being with Big Ma and Papa. She smiles the entire time, unless Baby Girl acts up. I guess all the fun we have there reminds her of the good times she had while growing up in the same house.

We run all over that big stretch of beautiful, glossy grass, from one end to other. While sitting under the different fruit trees and the fragrant floral trees, my little sisters and I pretend. We imagine all kind of things we will do and be when we grow up.

Of course, there is the fun of tire swing! The tire swing goes right over the center of the pond, if you push off hard enough. Then you let your hands go off the rope, and there you go—you have the biggest splash you ever felt!

Suddenly, my blissful thoughts while walking are interrupted. We hear sounds that slowly get louder, and they are louder than the crunching sounds that our feet are making on this gravel road. The sound is of horses coming from behind me. As I turn around to see, Baby Girl squeezes my hand a little tighter. Mama and Auntie move fast; they come around in front of me and are now facing the horses as they approach. Ruthie grabs Baby Girl's other hand, and we all stop. Mama has her walking stick, made from a big tree limb, that she always carries in case any big critters try to bother us along the way.

We usually don't run into anyone when we take this walk, especially on horses. Before we know it, three men dressed in fancy clothes approach us slowly on their horses, all of them glaring at Mama and Auntie. Mama and Auntie guide us to the side of the road so the men have room to get by and go about their business.

"Well, hello, ladies! How is your day going?" says one of the riders. He stands out among the three, wearing a black felt hat with a red feather in it. Surprisingly, his greeting is with a bright smile and in a kind and friendly tone.

"Just fine, sir, and yours?" Mama says, using her strong yet ladylike voice.

Mama has barely given her reply when one of the other riders—a man with a bald head and a beard that looks frazzled and unkempt—screams, "Where you gals headed out here on this road?"

Suddenly, there's a definite change in the way that Mama and Auntie are standing. We all look into each other's eyes, and Baby Girl squeezes my hand tighter, out of fear. We know our favorite day and walk might take a turn for the worse.

Auntie then says cheerfully, "We are going to our Ma and Pa's house, and we are running a little late, sir."

Then the third rider, wearing a blue bandana, rides slowly over to where we are standing. We have to move out of the way because he rides around Auntie two times, looking at her in a certain way. He stops right in front of her and yells, "How old are you, gal? You got a husband?"

Auntie looks down at the ground. Before she can answer, Mama says, "Yes, sir; she married two years now. They mighty pleased, sir, 'cause she in a family way."

"Is that so, gal?" he yells, staring at Auntie.

Ruthie is getting very upset; I can see her getting angrier by the minute. Tears stream down her face now, and before my auntie can answer the third horseman, Ruthie yells angrily, "We got to go now, sir! My papa is going to be looking for us. He might be here soon!"

"Shut your mouth, gal. Stay in your place—you hear?" he shouts back at her.

The anger rises even more in Ruthie as she reaches for Mama's walking stick, but Mama won't let go of her stick.

The rider with the felt hat rides over and puts himself and his horse between Auntie and the third rider "We are going to let you ladies be on your way now. You all have a good day," he says politely but firmly, looking straight at the rider who was so rude to Auntie.

The three men then turn their horses the way they were originally riding and go on their way.

Baby Girl reaches for me to carry her; she had started crying too. We walk very slowly until we can't see the three men ahead of us anymore. Ruthie walks in front of Mama and Auntie with her head down, often kicking the rocks on the ground, like she was kicking the head of the man who was so rude.

Mama always tells Ruthie not to be so quick-tempered. She just wants her to keep her mouth shut and let the grown folks handle things. Ruthie always tells Mama okay, but when she holds it in, that seems to make it worse.

Mama usually gives Ruthie a good tongue-lashing when she disobeys, but she is too busy calming Auntie down.

We walk on to Big Ma's in silence, but the tension is so thick I could cut it with a knife. It's a silence that's filled with our vulnerabilities, our helplessness, and the fear that comes from knowing that often, we have no control of what happens to our lives.

Big Ma tells us girls that someday, women will not have to worry about what people say or what they will do to us. Being strong in our hearts, minds, and souls, no matter what, is the key to women being fortunate in this life. That's what Big Ma says. She also says that when things happen, don't wait to pray to God; pray right away. We have been taught that God will do what we pray for, if we talk to Him and trust and believe in Him. Mama tells me not to lie—that is something that really displeases our Creator.

I decided I'll pray and communicate to God right now. I talk to my Creator in my head and heart, so no one can hear me as we are walking. "Well, God, I'm talking to You again. Can You fix it so Mama do not have to lie when we trying to take our favorite walk from now on? I know You know Auntie do not have a husband and no baby coming. Forgive, Mama, God. I don't want You to be displeased with her, but she had to help Auntie. Amen." There; I know everything is all right now.

I can tell Baby Girl has gone to sleep because she feels much heavier on my back. I am holding her tight with her arms around my shoulders. Just over the hill, and we will be there. Ruthie likes to run down the hill until she gets to the house. This is one of those moments, and there she goes, only this time, she is running as fast as she can. Mama and Auntie are laughing a little. Mama must have said something funny to cheer up Auntie. I am so glad we are here. I see our "brown family house," as Big Ma and Papa call it.

Big Ma takes turns making everyone's favorite sweet treat each week. My favorite is her strawberry cake. I wonder if that is what she's made. Oh, here comes Papa. He always looks for us so that he can meet us and carry Baby Girl the rest of the way for me. Ruthie stops running long enough to give Papa a big hug and then takes off running again to see Big Ma.

Papa always looks so handsome with his slightly bronzed skin and his jet-black hair, eyes, and moustache. Papa always wears the same type of clothes at the family house. His at-home attire is a white long-sleeve shirt with tan overalls. His shirt collar is always open. A white hankie hangs out of his right back pocket, and he's wearing a pair of Red Wing work boots.

"Hey, Papa," Mama and Auntie yell as he approaches us a little way off. Papa is close enough now where I can stop to rest and wait for him to take Baby Girl. She is in a deep sleep now.

"*Hesci. Estonko?*" Papa says as he walks past Mama and Auntie to relieve me of the weight of Baby Girl. "*Hesci. Estonko?*" means "Hello. How are you?" in one of the languages Papa grew up with, the Muscogee language, the language of his mother.

"We're doing just fine. Glad we're here," Auntie replies. She glances at Mama and me with a look that tells us, *Do not say anything about our encounter with those men on horseback.*

Gently taking Baby Girl off my back, my Papa says, "*Hesci. Estonko*, Peaches?"

Peaches is the special name my grandparents gave me. I am the first grandchild of Papa and Big Ma. When I was a baby, my grandparents say that I loved for them to feed me mashed peaches. The peaches came off their tree next to their house, and they would cook them just for me.

Oh, my back feels so much better with Baby Girl off it. Just as my back feels better after Baby Girl is off me, everything within me feels better, and everything is better when I hear my Papa say my name: Peaches.

Peaches—that is me, and I know that I am special, like my mama and grandparents have told me.

We can all read and write, and Big Ma and Papa have shown me in the Bible that I am an overcomer. Nothing will ever—not in my entire life—tear me down.

The Safe House

As soon as we are just a few steps from the front porch, I can smell Big Ma's delicious cooking. I can't tell what she's cooked, but I can smell her delicious fry bread for sure. Big Ma comes through the kitchen door down the hall, wiping her hands on her white apron and smiling like the sun is rising right there inside the house.

My Big Ma is the most beautiful woman in the world, besides my mama. Big Ma is a stout lady who always has a pleasant face, and she holds her head up, no matter what is going on, good or bad. She tells us to do the same because there was a time when she did not look pleasant or hold her head up. It was always down. I've never asked her why her head was always down; some things we do not ask the grown folks.

Today, she's wearing her pretty, navy, long-sleeve, small-collar blouse. It has rows of pleats all the way down the front to where there is a wide band around her waist, then more pleats down from the bottom of the band. Big Ma just loves prairie skirts; she has a lot of them in assorted colors and designs. She put on a navy-and-white floral prairie skirt today, as well as her beaded moccasins. Big Ma has a part in the center of her bangs, brushed to each side, and her long, thick, curly braid is wrapped around the back of her head. Big Ma has accented her attire with silver and turquoise jewelry, and it makes her look like the queen she is.

She belts out a jolly laugh. "Here's the rest of my flowers." She gives each of us a hug. "Are you all right? I heard you ran into some havoc on the way." Big Ma has a concerned look, and she puts her hands on her hips. Big Ma has beautiful brown skin, and when she is worried or upset, lines appear on her forehead, and her eyes get much larger than usual. Big Ma has that worried look right now.

"They're all right, just ready for some of that lemonade to satisfy their thirst," Papa says as he lays Baby girl down on the sofa in the living room off the entryway. He covers her with a blanket.

"That's not what Ruthie said. Some troublemakers showed up on their way, Papa," Big Ma says.

"Is that right?" Papa asks, looking at Auntie and Mama.

"We're all right Papa," Mama says, looking at Auntie.

Silence falls in the front hallway of that big house, and quickly, Big Ma says, "Well, we have plenty of time to chat. You girls go ahead and freshen up while I pour you each that nice cold lemonade your Papa is talking about. Go ahead now, so you can rest your feet."

That sounds so good, and as soon as I finish drinking it, I run down to the pond and stick these tired feet in the warm water that's waiting for me. I love this special place. There is a waterfall above the pond, and I love to hear the water from the fall hitting the pond.

Our day is wonderful, as usual. We all sit at the kitchen table, having cold lemonade and cornmeal cookies that have raisins and pecans in them. We laugh and catch up on the happenings of the past week. My mama shares that she is going to start back to work three days a week at the doctor's office in town. Auntie says she's going to take care of Baby Girl and the house while Mama is working and Ruthie and I are learning our lessons at the schoolhouse for five hours a day.

Big Ma says she bought everything in town the other day that we need to make more baskets for storage in her pantry and for our house. Big Ma also bought pretty string and beads to make more jewelry for our dolls.

Papa is unusually quiet and excuses himself to go out to the yard after sitting there for just a little bit. I know he's thinking about what Big Ma said about the troublemakers. I know they will talk about it when Ruthie, Baby Girl, and I are out playing. One thing I learned when I was little was not to ask grown folks about their business; stick with kid stuff. If it's about grown-ups, do not say one word, or I will be in big trouble.

Soon afterward, Ruthie, Baby Girl, and I are outside, sticking our feet in the pond again. After refreshing our feet, we run, jump, play hide-and-seek, and help Papa pick strawberries and put them in a basket. Papa takes the basket of strawberries into the house but does not come back out right away. Because it's a little cool from the rain, Mama says we cannot jump in the pond from the tire swing. When Papa comes back out with his fishing pole, we spend time helping him catch some fish.

I love catching fish with Papa, holding tight to the fishing pole, and the feeling when the fish gets on the hook. I do not like worms or touching them; that's Ruthie and Papa's part. Sometimes Ruthie chases me with a worm or two, but I'm a better runner than her, so she never catches me.

Time goes by so fast at the family house. This time, though, Mama says we can stay outside a little longer, which makes us ever so happy. We play so hard, and I laugh until my sides hurt. Every step Ruthie and I make has Baby Girl on our heels. She is getting faster now and does not cry as much when we play games. I hope she does not grow up too fast; I love being her second mommy.

We cannot get cleaned up for dinner fast enough. The good smell of Big Ma's cooking is throughout the house. All the food is on the big wooden table, and we are ready! There is so much on the table—beef stew, fried fish, collard greens, rice pudding, home-fried potatoes, corn on the cob, and Big Ma's delicious fry bread.

When Big Ma was growing up, her family had a tradition of getting together for Sunday dinner. It is particularly important to her and Papa, and she wants us to carry on the tradition when we have our families. We cannot always come to visit on Sundays, but Big Ma says it does not matter what the day is; if we see each other every week, that is all that matters. I laugh because she and Papa say that whatever day we visit is their Sunday.

Papa had the sun tea sitting on the porch bannister when we arrived. It fascinates Baby Girl how the tea glows and glitters as the bright sun hits it. It is perfect and delicious, served with this loved-filled meal. Ruthie makes a loud blowing sound as Auntie blesses the food—Auntie's prayers sometimes are little too long. Mama gives Ruthie "the eye" to tell her not to be so impatient. My sisters and I know what "the eye" means—it's the look Mama gives when she cannot verbalize to us to act right. The eye speaks louder than any words Mama can say, and she is not playing.

Supper is so good; there really is not much talking at the table. Papa says supper is not the time to talk but to eat, and with this tasty food, I do not have a problem with that. Ruthie and I help Auntie clear the table, clean the kitchen, and sweep the floors. Big Ma, Papa, and Mama are out on the front porch in their rocking chairs. Papa is smoking his pipe, Mama is watering the plants on the porch, and Big Ma is rocking Baby Girl in her lap. When we finish the chores in the kitchen, Mama and Auntie get the beads and string that Big Ma bought us so we can make jewelry for our dolls. Ruthie and I sit on the top step of the porch, working with our beads and dolls, as Mama and Auntie work on the baskets.

"Girls, how would you like to spend the night?" Mama says with a big grin.

"Really?" Ruthie says, looking at Mama, almost screaming with joy.

"Well, the sun will be going down before you get home, even if you left now," Big Ma says, looking up at the sky. "Besides, I want you to finish your dolls so I will know what kind of beads to buy next for your other projects. Papa has his business meeting in town again, so I'll ride in with him and do some more shopping."

My sisters and I rarely spend the night at the family house, so we are happy and each hug and kiss our grandparents. Papa and Big Ma are happy too because that is the second thing that they love the most from us—our hugs and kisses. The first and most important thing in our lives is for us to read our Bible, pray, and be obedient to our elders.

"We will have to go down to the pond to clean up, but first, go into my room. Each of you get your night clothes and your outfit for tomorrow out of the spare clothes drawer," Mama said firmly. "Lay your clothes neatly on the window seat, and on the way out of the room, get a chew-stick and a handful of mint from the herb basket to chew on until we get back from the springs."

"I'll go with you," Big Ma says happily. "Peaches, I will tend to Baby Girl at the springs, so you can get back to your beading."

Ruthie has already run into the house, gotten her things, and is off to the pond before I know it. *There she goes again*, I think, *always trying to be the first and to outdo me. I guess that's what little sisters do*. She should have waited until we could all leave together, but we are coming right behind her.

The rest of the night goes by fast. Down at the pond, we all clean up, except Big Ma; she cleans up Baby Girl. Auntie stays on the porch with Papa while we are down there. We are back quickly and work on our beads; Mama and Auntie on their baskets. Big Ma is rocking Baby Girl, and Papa is playing his flute. I look at the sky, and all I can see, no matter which way I turn, are bright stars; some are twinkling. I can also smell the strawberry cake in the oven that Big Ma made when we came back from the pond. Big Ma was going to make one of Ruthie's favorites, but Ruthie kept going back and forth and could not decide. Big Ma told Ruthie, "Think about it until you come back next week," and she baked my favorite instead.

We have to get up early, and Big Ma says we don't have any more playing time. Papa tells us a story, as he always does when we sit on the porch. I cannot think of one time when I've sat on this porch that Papa did not tell a wonderful story. We laugh and talk, and I know we have to go to bed soon. Baby Girl is almost asleep in Big Ma's lap, and Papa starts playing his flute again, only this time, he plays a slow song—a song he plays just as much as he tells his stories. I realize, sitting there, that as far back as I can remember my grandparents, Papa has played that song every time.

I look at Mama and ask, "Mama, does Papa have a name for that song? It sounds so good to me. It always has."

Mama sits down next to me and put her arms around me. "This is an incredibly special song, Peaches. Big Ma wrote it." She looks directly in my eyes and says quite seriously, "I like it too, and I want you girls to remember it all your lives." She gives me a tight squeeze, and Papa keeps on playing, but much softer, as Big Ma says, "'Engraved in His Palm.'"

I look back at Big Ma. "'Engraved in His Palm'?"

"Yes, 'Engraved in His Palm.' That's the name of it," my mama says, with her arms still hugging me tightly. "Big Ma wrote it for our family. It has powerful words to it too, Peaches. I am going to teach you girls the words, OK?"

Ruthie then chirps, "We don't want Peaches to sing it. She sounds terrible when she sings!"

"Ruthie," Big Ma says with a stern yet gentle voice.

I look back at Ruthie and roll my eyes at her. *Leave it to her to spoil a rare family moment*, I think. *I don't know why Ruthie must always spoil things. Ugh! She is so mean.* "Yes, Mama, I want to learn the song. Maybe Papa can teach me how to play it on the flute since my voice isn't so good."

Ruthie starts laughing uncontrollably. Papa stops playing the flute. Mama then looks at Ruthie with "the eye," and Ruthie stops laughing immediately. Mama looks at me with such love in her eyes and says. "Peaches, your voice is beautiful. Everything about you is beautiful. Do you know why?"

Thinking before I reply, I smile at her and say, "Yes, Mama, I do know why. It's because our Creator made me, and I am wonderfully made—unique—because He loves me. He loves me so much that He will never leave me or forget about me, no matter what happens in my life."

"That's right, Peaches, and don't you ever forget it!" Papa says. Then he starts playing "Engraved in His Palm" all over again, a little louder, as Mama starts teaching the words. Big Ma gets up to put Baby Girl to bed, and Ruthie is right on Big Ma's heels. She knows Mama is not through with her yet for saying I can't sing.

Mama, Papa, and I stay on the porch for a while after everyone else is tucked in for the night. I love being with Papa and Mama in this moment, just the three of us, looking at the stars. I want the night to last forever, but my eyes cannot stay open. Big Ma comes out on the porch and whispers in my ear. "Time to go to sleep, my Peaches. We've got an early start."

"Yes, Yes Big Ma," I say very sleepily.

It's not difficult to get up the next morning—I slept so hard and so well. It feels great to stay all night at the family house, wake up, and still be here. We sit at the table on the other end of the front porch, where Big Ma and Papa eat breakfast and have their morning coffee, when the weather permits. There are always fresh-picked flowers in a vase in the middle of the table, on top of a hard-pressed linen tablecloth. We eat oatmeal with butter, honey, and blueberries in it. Along with it, we have toast with peach preserves, bacon, and buttermilk. *More yummies for my tummy*, I think as I sit at the table.

Papa finishes his breakfast first. As he stands up, he announces that he will take us home today.

"We don't have to walk today, Papa?" Ruthie asks, with concern on her face.

"No, you will not walk anymore when you come to the family house, nor will you walk home when you go back to your other house. Big Ma and I will come pick you up and take you home from now on," Papa says very seriously.

Papa has a new carriage in the big shed out back. He has not used it very often since he bought it. Papa and Big Ma are very adamant about neighbors not knowing their business, especially any achievements or progress. It might bring too much attention to them, and they don't want any trouble.

Big Ma and Papa had talked about having a carriage for a long time. Big Ma wanted one very much. She said that when she and Papa went to town, she didn't feel like a lady by the time they got there, between her perspiring and all the dust that got on her. She knew she couldn't do it anymore. Papa was not too keen on buying it at first, but Big Ma eventually convinced him. She told Papa that it also would be helpful when they go to town for supplies and convenient for our family. She also explained that she was getting older, and it was too much for her to walk or ride the horse anymore. I think that's what really convinced Papa; he doesn't want Big Ma to hurt herself.

Big Ma and Papa have a lot of wonderful things, and they share those things with us and everyone else who needs them—food, clothes, quilts, plants; whatever my grandparents have, they will share. Papa and Big Ma say, "What we have, you have. It's all ours together." Papa, Big Ma, Mama, and Auntie have taught us that God gives us all that we have, and because God gives to us, we are to give to others—that's the best and only way to live. Because we are givers, we will never lack anything we need. Most of the time, there is no lack for what we want either. Our grandparents say we could never have all that we have if it was left up to our thoughts, abilities, and actions. Papa says we are not smart enough, especially with the situations and circumstances our family has. Only our Creator can put us on a safe path and keep us on that safe path. To be thankful to God by telling Him and showing Him thanks daily is more important than receiving all that He gives us. I wonder what family "situations and circumstances" Papa is talking about. I will just have to wonder because there is no way I'm asking my elders. Ruthie would ask, but I am leaving grown folks' business alone. I don't want to be the receiver of the eye or have them feel I am not obedient.

Papa says when our hands are closed tight, we cannot give or receive anything. Now, we benefit again from the love of my grandparents and will not have to take those long walks anymore. Ruthie, Baby Girl, and I are so excited because we have never ridden in a carriage! While Mama and Big Ma are getting things together for our ride, Auntie tells me she is not going back with us today but will return in two days. Sometimes, my aunt Candy, who is also Big Ma's sister but much older than Mama and Auntie, comes to visit. When Aunt Candy comes to the family house, Auntie stays over to help her and Big Ma. My two aunties help Big Ma with farming chores and the general cleaning of the house, and they cook and preserve foods for the winter months. The end of the summer and fall are when Big Ma and her love team are the busiest. By the end of October and early November, it is just too cold for that type of work.

Papa is our protector; he does all the hunting and the hard chores on the land, and he cares for the horses and other animals in the barn. Aunt Candy is coming tomorrow to help. I love when Aunt Candy comes because her daughter, my cousin Arlee, comes along with her most of the time. Arlee and I are cousins, but we are also best friends. We both were born in the same year—1918—but Arlee is four months older than me. I only have five more weeks and then we both will be eight years old. Mama and Aunt Candy always have us celebrate our birthdays together. I don't know why, but one of the family's most important occasions is my and Arlee's birthdays. It is always a wonderful time. Arlee and I are very close—like twins! Been like that since we both can remember.

Over the years, we usually have shared one birthday cake at the family gatherings, but this year, we each will have our own cake. Since we will be eight, we eat a lot more than we did when we were little. Most of the family will come to celebrate. We will need two big three-layer cakes, all right; our family loves to eat!

"Aw, I thought you were going to ride with us in Papa's carriage," I say to Auntie, feeling a little disappointed. I love for Auntie to be around us all the time, and I miss her when she is not home with us.

"Peaches, we will have lots of times to ride together," Auntie says. "We are so lucky that we don't have to walk anymore. Don't talk about the carriage at the schoolhouse or to other people. It's family business—only family—OK?"

"Yes, Auntie," I reply quickly.

The adults in my family are so sensitive about other people knowing what's going on with us. I don't know why, and unlike Ruthie, I am not trying to find out. I don't want Mama upset with me.

Auntie then sits down next to me and says that Big Ma and Papa are considered well-to-do by people who live around them and the people in and around the town.

"What's 'well-to-do'?" I ask Auntie.

"That's when people work hard, make money lawfully, spend their money only when they have to, and save rest of their money. We only spend money for things that the family needs to live on. When everything goes well with saving the money, they use it for emergency situations, family members who need help, and investments," Auntie explained. "That's how Papa got the money to buy everything needed to build our big family house. Papa also had to pay workers to help him because he a wanted a house so that no one in the family ever would be without a place to stay."

Auntie says, "When Papa was younger, he didn't have a home for a long time."

"Why didn't Papa have a home?" I ask. "Wasn't he with his mama and daddy?"

Auntie hesitates when I ask her that. Her smile leaves her face, and then, as she looks away, she says, "You have to ask your mama about that, Peaches. I'm sure she'll tell you. It's her place to do that." Auntie seems like she wants to tell me more but does not.

I felt so sad when I heard that. I can't imagine my wonderful Papa not having a place to stay. He is always is so kind and loving. He makes everything so nice for everybody and helps however he can. Papa is an expert at making things better for people, and he has been teaching me how to be the same. *Papa is so happy. He never looks or acts like there was a time when he didn't have a home,* I think.

Auntie must have seen that the information about Papa is heart-wrenching for me, and before I can dwell on it for very long, she says, "You know what else Papa and Big Ma did with some of their savings?"

"What did they do?" I ask, eager to know.

"Well, they hired a teacher Papa found out about. Her name was Miss Peterson from over on the other side of town. Miss Peterson would come and teach your mama and me from all kinds of books we'd read. She'd teach us to write properly and learn all our school lessons while we were growing up," Auntie says cheerfully.

"Really? You and Mama didn't go to the schoolhouse?" I ask.

Auntie's smile leaves her face again, and she speaks slower than usual. "Well, during that time we did not go to the schoolhouse. We had private lessons. Anyway, Papa and Big Ma felt that we should have our lessons at home instead of somewhere else." Auntie has said this with a look like she wants to say so much more.

As I get older, I am learning a few things about my family, but when I learn something, I end up with even more questions. At least there is a chance Arlee will visit, and we can talk about it. We talk about everything. I keep her secrets, and she keeps mine. She wants to have a life like Big Ma and Papa too. That's why we say we are twins—we were born close together and think the same.

The ride back is exciting for us. Big Ma rides with us also. The carriage is bigger than Ruthie and I thought it would be, especially when Papa pulls it in front of the porch. It has four *huge* wheels, two in the front and two in the back. There is a frame of some sort that connects the carriage and the two horses together.

A huge, thick leather strap goes into the frame and around the horses in the front. It runs on top of the horses for a long way, straight into Papa's hands. That way, the carriage, horses, and Papa are all connected.

Papa sits directly behind the horses in a double seat that is up very high. This seat has room for another person to sit to the right of Papa. On top, behind Papa, are two more rows of double seats for four more people to sit on and bars on the side to hold on to. Below is the actual carriage, with shiny, heavy black doors on each side with strong brass handles and two steps on each side to help passengers enter the inside of the carriage. Inside the carriage are double seats again, on each side of the carriage, facing each other; these seats, though, are fancy black leather. Blue fabric is on the walls and ceiling. The fabric has shiny white-rope trim, with two very fancy tacks at each end that hold the fabric down. A wooden floor, painted shiny black, and the windows on the carriage leave us all amazed.

Papa and Big Ma have their dress clothes on. They are going to town after we get home, and they look very smart. As much as I love the carriage, I look at the seats that are on the top, and I feel a little afraid. *What if I fall off? They are awfully high!* Ruthie is all for it, though. She puts her foot on the step on the side to get up top, but Mama says, "No, Ruthie, Papa and Big Ma said you girls cannot ride behind Papa on the seats up top until you are ten or twelve years old, depending on your size at that time."

Whew! I feel relieved. I was truly scared to get way up there! Of course, Ruthie has her objections and is fussing and carrying on, saying she's not a baby but a big girl.

"Get your butt in that carriage, girl!" Auntie screams from the top of the porch. "Don't make me come down there and put you in that carriage myself, Ruthie."

Ruthie looks very annoyed. Papa comes around to help us in, and, with much protest, Ruthie climbs in first. Papa helps Big Ma up into the carriage, smiling at her. Then Papa helps Baby Girl get into Big Ma's lap. I carefully step into the carriage, with

Papa's help, and sit next to Ruthie. I have a great feeling of relief that we don't have to walk anymore. I start reliving the encounter with those men who came upon us on the way to our visit here. I was very scared, but being the oldest, I could not show my fear, especially with Ruthie already mad and crying. Baby Girl always needs me to be strong too because she is extremely sensitive, and she clings to me a lot. I am working hard to be like Mama, Auntie, and Big Ma, who are always extraordinarily strong and have great trust in our Creator.

What would have happened if the man with the black hat and red feather had not been so kind to us and had not protected us from the other two men? What if Ruthie had grabbed Mama's walking stick? She must stop being so quick-tempered. What would have happened to Auntie and Mama? How could I have helped them if I had Baby Girl, and Ruthie was out of control?

Mama is standing on the other side of the carriage with the door open, looking in at me. "Peaches, honey, are you OK?" Mama can always read me; it's like she knows what I am thinking sometimes.

"Yes, Mama, I'm fine."

She gives me a look and a smile that says *I love you* without saying a word, and I feel better. I smile back at her, and she knows I'm all right again. Looking at Ruthie and Baby Girl, she says, "You girls behave yourselves. Don't give Big Ma and Peaches a tough time on this ride back, you hear me?"

"Yes, Mama," Baby Girl says.

Ruthie does not respond. She looks at Mama, sees "the eye," and quickly says, "Yes, Mama."

"All right, then. I'm riding up top with Papa. We'll be there before we know it since we are riding and not walking." Mama said this as she glanced at me. She winks her eye at me, and I smile at her again as she and Papa close the doors to the carriage on each side at the same time. We can't see them, but I can hear them up top, getting ready for us to take off. Auntie comes to the window of the carriage and throws kisses at us; then, she stands back as we pull off. At that moment, my heart is so full of love and security because of the family that God put me into. Mama tells us that God always makes a way of escape for us, no matter what we go through, and we can count on that.

Big Ma talks to us as we start on the ride. She is so happy that she and Papa finally got their carriage. "One day," she says, "when Papa doesn't have to take care of business anymore, we are thinking of helping the folks in the county with rides in the carriage for wherever they must go." Big Ma is happy when she talks about it because, she says, she and Papa will never have to be apart.

The ride is fun and bumpy, but with every bump, we laugh. The harder the bump, the harder we laugh. After a while, Baby Girl rubs her eyes and quickly is fast asleep. We can hear Mama and Papa talking but can't tell what they are saying. They seem to be enjoying the ride as much as we are because we can hear them laughing as well. Before long, Ruthie goes to sleep too, with her head on my shoulder in a rare and tender moment. I love my pretend-to-be-tough younger sister. Even though she gets on my nerves, I cannot imagine my life without her in it.

Now Big Ma's eyes are closed, but I don 't know if she is asleep yet. Sometimes, she closes her eyes when she is thinking hard or when she is talking to our Creator. Looking out the window, I see the place where we were approached by the three men. Just looking at it makes my heart beat fast, especially as we pass through, and I feel like I'm going to throw up my breakfast. My heart slows down the farther away we get from that awful spot. It dawns on me what Mama said about God making a way of escape! God has used this carriage and my grandparents to escape what could have been horrible situations for my family.

No longer do we have to experience the uncertainty of *if* we will make it to the family house or what kind of condition we would be in if we got there. I then think, *What if we run into them on this ride?* But that thought leaves right away because Papa, sitting on top, has a big shotgun on the floor by his feet. Yep, Papa is our protector.

The last thing I remember about our first carriage ride before I fall asleep is hearing my mama's happy laughter with Papa above us. My stomach is feeling better, and as I stare at the trees with glossy leaves, my eyes get heavy. I too go to sleep, like my younger sisters, feeling relieved again that we were not walking, feeling so safe, and feeling extremely loved.

Flawed Treasures

Busy at our house, Ruthie and I are cleaning up the living room. Ruthie dusts the furniture, while I sweep the wooden floor. Our house isn't as large as Papa and Big Ma's family house, but it has enough room for all of us. There is me, my sisters, Mama, my daddy, and, of course, my sweet auntie. I miss Auntie already. Big Ma and Papa haven't been gone long, and already it seems like a day.

My daddy works at night for the railroad, so we don't see him much. Mama says he works too much and too hard and hasn't had a good rest in a long time. That is why she is going back to work, so Daddy doesn't have to work so much. Daddy does not want Mama to work; he prefers that she stay with us girls. When he comes home, he cleans up, eats the meal Mama prepares for him, and sleeps all day. Later in the night, right after dark, Daddy gets up, eats again, and goes off to work with his jacket and lunch bag in hand. That is the life Daddy lives, and he says he doesn't mind living it that way because he wants us to have what we need.

I know he also wants us to have special surprises too, things we don't have to have but are nice to have. Sometimes, he gives Mama extra money to buy us things. Some of the surprises that Daddy has had Mama buy for us are beautiful dresses, nice school clothes, pretty ribbons for our hair, special shoes, and warm stockings. He also has bought us each a little bear, and we all have dolls with golden hair. Baby Girl sleeps with her bear; sometimes Ruthie does too. Ruthie won't admit she sleeps with her bear; she thinks she is too tough for that.

Daddy says he buys us surprises because he wants us to know how much he loves us. I think Daddy feels bad that he cannot be around that much. Daddy says that his father worked a lot too so that all the family's needs would be met and so the family would be able to live together under the same roof. That is all Daddy ever says about his parents and how he grew up. He also tells us girls not to ask any questions; all the adults tell us that. How are we to know about anything if we can't ask questions? It is very strange; I cannot figure out why we cannot know things.

Mama says Daddy is such a hard worker because it was difficult for Daddy and his family when he was younger. Mama wants me to understand Daddy better. She sees that, at times, he is very annoying to me.

Recently, Mama said she wanted to tell me something about my daddy.

"It's a secret," she said, "and it has to stay between just the two of us." Mama's secret was that my daddy's father was a slave.

"A *slave*? What's a slave?" I asked Mama. I'd never heard of such a thing. It turns out that a slave is a human being that is for sale; someone who is purchased by a buyer and is then a possession to perform work duties for the buyer. Slaves are not considered total human beings and cannot live their lives the way they want to live. They cannot live where they want to live, go where they want to go, or work where they want to work. They must obey the owner and do everything the owner tells them to do.

My daddy's father was for sale and was bought and owned by someone called the master. I thought God, the Creator, was the only one called Master! Turns out, there were a lot of masters, but there is a significant difference between that kind of master and our Master, God, the Creator. Mama explained that my grandfather, Daddy's father, was not born on this land we live on. My grandfather was born far, far away. The way Mama explained it was like this: men went to the land where my grandfather, then a young teen, and his family lived. These men took my grandfather, his father, his sister, and his uncle away. His uncle was my grandfather's mother's brother, not his father's brother. My grandfather and my great-grandfather did not want to leave their land, nor did his sister and uncle. Even though they did not want to leave, my father's family were captured and forced by men with guns onto a huge boat. Mama said that it was not a pleasant trip on the boat, that it was horrible and nothing like when Papa takes us out on the water in the family canoe.

These men had my grandfather and great-grandfather lying down on their backs on a rack with other people who also had been captured. The captured men were all chained to each other on the racks in the bottom of the boat. Mama said the trip lasted for an extremely long time.

This secret was so shocking to me that I could hardly swallow. It felt like I had a big lump in my throat. The family was separated from each other on the boat, except for my grandfather and great-grandfather. They lay next to each other, chained together. Despite the severity of the situation, Grandfather and my great-grandfather were still hopeful they would find a way to unite with the sister and uncle and return home.

I do not know what happened on that boat on the way to this land, but my great-grandfather died, lying right next to his son, my daddy's daddy. Mama said she did not know what my great-grandfather was sick with that caused him to die; there was no way to know under the conditions. When it was time to remove my great-grandfather's body, the boat workers unchained my grandfather to help.

My grandfather, carrying his father to the top of the ship, was relieved that he was the one to care for his father's body. My daddy wasn't sure why, but it appeared to my grandfather that the boat did not have a holding place for deceased passengers. When my grandfather got to the top of the boat, the men insisted that my grandfather throw his father's body into the water, but he refused to do it. Because of his refusal to dishonor his father in death, my grandfather was stabbed in the arm by one man, while another took his father's body and threw him overboard.

My grandfather told Daddy that he didn't remember much about the rest of the trip after that. He was savagely beaten before he was taken back down and chained again. After that devasting experience, my grandfather became ill and was close to death. Through all this turmoil, my grandfather remained alive. His goal was to reunite with his sister and uncle and take them back to their home.

Daddy told this story to Mama twice, and she said that both times, he never went any further; he just could not continue. He wept both times he spoke about it. Mama might not have realized it, but when she spoke to me about it, her voice was cracking, and tears were streaming down her face. Seeing Mama cry released the tears I was holding back as I listened, and we cried together. To think that my grandfather and great-grandfather were mistreated so badly just broke my heart. I felt so hurt about my great-aunt and uncle too.

I wonder what happened to them. I hope they were not beaten and treated badly or killed. I am a big girl now, and I know when the people I love are hurting badly. I can see that the story Daddy shared with Mama about his family was just as painful for her, so I gave her a big hug and thanked her for trusting me with the secret. I promised Mama that I would not be so critical of Daddy and would not allow myself to get annoyed so easily. It has not been that long since we talked about it. I do want to find out more about my grandfather and my other family members. It is sad to think he was separated from his family. I do not know what I would do without my family—to be somewhere without them, all alone. I am not going to think about that, ever.

Ruthie and I finish cleaning the living room. *I better concentrate on the other chores*, I think. I help Mama set the table for Daddy. She always makes it exactly right for him. I always get the mason jar—so he can have a jarful of water with his meal—and a clean, fresh linen napkin. When there are flowers in the yard, sometimes we put them in the center of the table, like Big Ma's porch table. We are through before we know it, and we go to sit on our back porch. We watch the squirrels run back and forth. Baby Girl likes to try to chase them, but, of course, she never catches them. Mama and I are sitting on the back step of our little porch. It isn't big enough for even one chair, but to me, that does not matter. I love the way Mama and I sit out here. This is the time when it is just her and me, and I treasure it. As we sit here, I want to get the nerve up to ask her why Papa did not have a home to live in when he was younger. Will she get annoyed with me, and give me the eye to let me know not to ask?

I don't say anything; before I can ask her, Mama starts singing the song that Big Ma wrote.

"Safe within. Safe within. Feels so good safe within. Within Your palm, within Your palm, I am engraved within Your palm." This is one of Mama's favorite songs; she loves to sing it. She sings whenever she is cleaning or in the garden. I start singing with Mama since I know the words now. It does not matter if she is happy or sad; Mama is going to sing. Mama and I are learning to sing this song together. No matter how it sounds, we love it. It's our song now. Singing this song makes Mama feel good, and when Mama feels good, I feel good. This is our song, and we feel wonderful when singing it together.

Mama keeps smiling, full of pleasure, as we sing together. We are interrupted by the sound of Daddy coming through the front door. Mama pats the top of my hand, her way to let me know we will finish our song later, as she rises from the porch to greet Daddy. I follow Mama in the house.

Mama looks at Daddy, smiling brightly, and says, "How are you doing? You have a good night?"

"It was all right. How's everybody?" Daddy says in a short, snappish voice.

Mama's smile leaves right away. She quickly glances at me and then looks back at Daddy. "Daddy doesn't mean any harm," Mama says. "He just needs to get more rest."

We must be patient and show him kindness and love the way Mama wants us to.

"Going to clean up now. Peaches, you all right?" Daddy says, speaking to me in a more pleasant voice.

"Yes, sir," I say, sitting at the kitchen table. Mama gives me a look that indicates I should let him be; he's tired. So I don't say anything about what happened to us on the walk to the family house or about the new family carriage and our ride home. I really want to tell Daddy about those men. They scared me like I never have been scared before. Here I go again, staying close-mouthed. Ugh.

Mama heats up Daddy's food and checks on Baby Girl and Ruthie while Daddy cleans up. Ruthie is reading a storybook to Baby Girl, and I listen, looking at Mama occasionally.

Mama is so smart; I want to be smart like her when I grow up. She knows a lot. She is teaching me that there will be a time when I will have to figure things out for myself, which I am looking forward to doing. When I have children and grandchildren, I will tell them anything that they want to know so they don't have to wonder about this and that. It just isn't fair. I will not forget to ask Mama about Papa and why he didn't have a home when he was young. It still hurts my feelings when I think about it. Now that I have learned about my grandfather and great-grandfather from Africa, that hurts too.

Daddy eats his meal, and, as usual, he doesn't say much. I sit at the table with Mama and Daddy as they talk about the new family carriage. Daddy is happy about our family carriage and seems relieved we do not have to walk to the family house anymore. Surprisingly, he seems relieved, even though he didn't know about the men on the road. Ruthie hears Mama talking, and she and Baby Girl come in because they also enjoyed the ride. Of course, this isn't the time for us girls to talk; it's grown folks' time in the kitchen. We know to be quiet if we want to stay in the room.

Mama says to Daddy, "You'll see it tomorrow morning, when Papa brings Missy back."

"Good," Daddy says, sounding exhausted.

Mama then says to Daddy, "Tomorrow is my appointment with Dr. Miller, so Misty will be here with the girls while you are getting your rest."

Daddy was drinking out of his mason jar when Mama said that to him. Now, he slams the mason jar down so hard that all of us girls jump, and Mama does too. Looking truly angry at Mama, Daddy says, "I told you, Colleen, you are not going back to that doctor's office to work. Why are you trying to aggravate me, and I just got home after working all night?"

Ruthie looks at Daddy and Mama, rolls her eyes at both of them, and walks out of the kitchen. Baby Girl climbs up in my lap, as Mama says to Daddy in a stern voice, "I am going to do what I need to do to help you and our family. If you keep working all these hours like this, you're going to kill yourself." Mama had moved closer to Daddy as she said this.

"You don't tell me what you are going to do," Daddy screams at Mama. "I am the man of this house, and you are going to do what I tell you!"

"Hubert, Misty will be here with Baby Girl, and, like always, the girls will be at the schoolhouse most of the time I am gone, so everything will be fine." Mama is trying to keep a patient tone.

Daddy looks at Mama with look on his face that I have seen before, a look that makes me feel like there is another person in this house with us and not my daddy. "What did I say?" Daddy says to Mama in a muffled voice, still with the stranger's face on.

"Hubert, listen to me," Mama says, but Daddy cuts her off by knocking everything on the table in front of him onto the floor— Daddy's plate, the mason jar, the vase on the table, everything!

Daddy screams at Mama, "We are not going to have our home out of order so folks can come in and say what happens with my family!"

Mama screams back at Daddy at the top of her lungs, "No

one is going to do that, Hubert. That's not going to happen! You cannot stop me from what I want to do. I am a grown woman, and I am able to help you out!"

By this time, Baby Girl is crying, and I am up from my chair, holding her, when, with one blow to Mama's face with the back of his hand, Daddy knocks Mama against the kitchen sink. I see Mama pick up a bowl off the sink and throw it at Daddy, and that's when Baby Girl and I take off running to the cedar closet in our bedroom. We squeeze in the closet. I sit down with Baby Girl on my lap and close the closet door as fast as I can. The distance makes a difference as far as what we can see, but it certainly doesn't make a difference in what we hear. The screaming and all the banging are as loud as if we are still in the kitchen. I hold my Baby Girl as close as I can. Baby Girl is crying so hard and sobbing, while covering her ears with her hands. The two of us huddle up together tightly on the hard cedar-closet floor. We listen in fear and terror to our parents go at each other—again. It's a feeling I cannot put into words, but then, I've never said anything to anyone about it.

It never happens when Auntie is here. I don't think she knows. If Auntie knew, I think she would tell Big Ma and Papa. I don't know what I will do if Daddy and Mama kill each other. I should not have sat at the table. I should have just let them have grown folks' time. If I had done that, then maybe they wouldn't fight. I have to get Baby Girl to calm down. She is so upset that she might want to pee. No, no, we are not leaving this closet. It's our safe place. I don't want her to be afraid. I don't want her to feel this despair that I am feeling right now.

Slowly, I begin rocking Baby Girl as I whisper in her ear, "It's all right. We are all right. God is with us, Baby Girl. You can't see Him, but He is right here with us." I squeeze her with all the love I feel in my heart for her. Why is this happening to us again? Why can't Daddy just accept Mama working? Or why can't Mama just do what Daddy wants? If they didn't have to take care of us, they would not do this to each other.

Baby Girl calms down, even though we still can hear the horrible chaos coming from the front of the house. Baby Girl looks up into my eyes, and I see a little assurance in what I said to her. I don't know how she can feel that way because I certainly don't feel that way at this moment. I smile at her and put her hair back in place—it looked wild after all the activity of getting into the closet.

I ask her, "Baby Girl, you want to play our pretend game?"

Baby Girl looks a little excited as she nods.

Acting like I am the most confident person in the world, I say, "Let's close our eyes, and let's pretend we are lying on our backs on the grass at the family house. We are right by the pond. We can hear the birds chirping, and we can hear the water. Are you there with me, Baby Girl?"

Baby Girl squeezes her eyes tight and squeezes my hand tighter as she whispers, "Yes, Peaches. I am there at Big Ma and Papa's with you."

"OK, let's look up in the sky and see what shape the angels made in the big buttermilk clouds today. Remember when we saw that cloud that looked like a puppy? Let's look in the clouds and see what we find today. Are you ready, Baby Girl?" I said this using an adventurous tone because I want to drown out the noise in the kitchen.

Baby Girl is happy to have a diversion and quickly starts playing our game of pretend. Every now and then, her body shakes, and she makes an uncontrollable snorting sound from her nose and mouth because she had been crying so hard. Mama had put a box of our handkerchiefs on the closet floor. I reach over and manage to get one so Baby Girl can blow her nose and wipe her face. She's happy just a little because the hankie is from a special box, with hankie selections made by Big Ma for Ruthie and me to use when we're away at the schoolhouse. Baby Girl has her own box of handkerchiefs, which she's had since she was born, so this hankie makes her feel like she's a big girl.

We play the pretending game for what seems like a long time.

I agree with Baby Girl on whatever she sees in the sky. She sees a ribbon, a flower, and Papa's flute. I tell her my discoveries as well, to keep the game going and continue to distract her. I start to feel distraught and desperate. I need something to counteract the noise that continues to take place, longer than our pretending game. We heard crashes and Mama and Daddy screaming and using harsh words. Mama was crying, and then there was a giant boom! The noise stops for a minute or two, and then Mama starts screaming again.

Then we hear Ruthie scream, "Stop! Stop! Why are you doing this again? Please stop!" We can tell that Ruthie starts crying after her pleas. "Daddy, if you hit Mama again, I'm going to hurt you!"

Mama screams, "Ruthie! Ruthie!"

We hear Daddy say, "Get on out of here. You have no business coming in here with that foolishness, and don't talk to me like that!"

Ruthie screams at Daddy, "You the one who got foolishness! Everything is good until you come home, and you always spoil things! You make us not want to see you come home! I wish you would never come back here and leave us alone!"

There is nothing but silence outside the closet at this point. We have waited for silence since we've been here in our little shelter. The silence we hear was going to be our sign that it was safe to come out, that the storm was over. Somehow, the reality of Ruthie's words cut straight to my heart, and it feels worse than any of the yelling and chaos did. This silence we hear is saying so much to our hearts and minds. It is cold, filled with hopelessness, with unanswered questions and an uncertain future. Baby Girl cries silently so no one outside our safe place can hear. She's trembling and biting her big-girl hankie. Sadness fills my heart, and I know it's not time for Baby Girl and me to exit the cedar closet.

I hold Baby Girl close to my chest so she can't see the tears I no longer can hold back. "Safe within, safe within. Feels so good safe within. Within Your palm, within Your palm, I'm engraved within Your palm" I rock and sing Big Ma's song repeatedly, hoping that will bring some type of comfort

t and peace to this little broken girl I hold.

Now, there's no more screaming, yelling, or glass breaking. Only the sounds of Mama and Ruthie sweeping up glass, cleaning up the kitchen, and going back and forth out the back door to the trash.

Baby Girl's eyes are starting to get heavy. I want to lay her on the bed, but I don't want to come out of my comfortable place of peace, so I just continue to rock and sing. What just happened to my family? Why did Ruthie say that to Daddy? Why did Mama keep talking and making Daddy mad? Did she forget about the mercy and kindness she told me about?

Baby Girl is in a deep sleep. I'm tired too. I am going to rest my eyes for a moment. Just going to rest my eyes.

**MH (Mental Health) A state of well being
mentally and all it encompasses.**

**MHC (Mental Health Condition) A illness
that affects an individual's thinking,
feelings, mood and behavior.**

MHC Trigger: Colleen and family confronted by men on the road while walking to her grandparents' home.

MHC Trigger: The treatment and the trauma that Colleen's Grandfather Spencer and Great-Grandfather Spencer and other family members experienced in being forcibly taken away from their home in Africa; being placed in inhuman conditions without their loved one's knowledge; the disposal of great-grandfather's remains and the trauma of these events being passed for three generations.

MHC Trigger: Colleen's parents argue and fight in the presence and within earshot of their three daughters.

Scriptural Support

For the mountains shall depart and the hills be removed, but my kindness shall not depart from you, Nor shall My covenant of peace be removed says the Lord who has mercy on you. (Isaiah 54:10 NKJV)

Finally, my brethren, be strong in the Lord and in the power of His might. (Ephesians 6:10 NKJV)

CHAPTER 2

Solid Ground

———⟫◆⟪———

There is nothing like waking up on my own. To sleep and not have anyone calling my name or shaking my arm until I open my eyes is simply fine with me. Lying here on the bed, it feels so good to rest my head on this soft pillow, with my comfortable, warm blanket covering me. I can hear and smell the activity taking place in the kitchen. It is Saturday morning, and I can lie here for as long as I care to. I have waited all week for this, and I am going to enjoy every minute.

I can hear Big Ma go out the door into the yard, getting fresh eggs for breakfast. I know she is happy that she slept in as well, but she is always the first one up; that's just the way it is. During the week, I stay terribly busy—it's expected of me, Being thirteen now, my responsibilities have increased greatly. My sisters and I have lived with Big Ma and Papa for five years now. Papa picks Mama and Auntie up for the weekends and takes them to work on Monday mornings, after he drops us girls off at the schoolhouse.

We are always happy when Mama and Auntie get here. Mama has been working with Dr. Miller for five years now as well, and they have recently moved to a fancy new office. Mama looks so pretty when she goes to work in her white uniform and her hair in a big bun. Auntie has a job near Mama; she is a secretary for an insurance company. Auntie wears the latest outfits—she likes that, especially her shoes with a higher heel.

Big Ma says it's important for us girls all to have a legitimate skill so we can get a good-paying job. We should get a skill so we won't have to do physically hard work. Mama says that Nana (Big Ma's mother) told her that we need jobs that pay better and will not eventually tear our bodies down.

Nana made sure that these facts were passed on to each generation. Nana did not have it easy. She worked in the fields as a child, and when she was older, she had problems with her back and feet. Mama says that years of work caused Nana to have trouble with walking later in life, and before she died, she could not walk at all. The elders have taught us that in our family, because of who we are and with our specific circumstances in life, it is a very a difficult goal to achieve employment that is not physically strenuous. That is why reading, writing, and progressing in education, as far as we can go in any school, is what we need to do to obtain that goal.

Papa and Big Ma say that one day, no matter who we are or where we come from, we will be able to get the highest education possible. We are told to strive for the highest education possible, and if, for some reason, we think we cannot reach that goal, we should keep trying. We are taught to do the best we can because God is faithful and will help us. These are the things that the women and men in my family have been told for generations. This way, eventually, we should be able to achieve what all people can achieve educationally, and that way, we will be treated as fairly as others.

Auntie gets off work an hour earlier than Mama, so she walks to Mama's job and waits until Mama is finished. Daddy still works for the railroad, only not as much as he used to work. Now, he works Sunday night through Thursday night, and he rests on Fridays and Saturdays. Mama and Auntie get a ride home from Auntie 's boyfriend, Joseph. Auntie says Joseph is not her boyfriend, that they are just friends. Whenever Auntie says that, Big Ma and Mama smile, and Mama winks at me.

I am glad that Mama and Auntie have a ride home, because they are safe and have protection.

The Talk and Facts

Growing up these past years, I have found out things that I was too young to understand before. It was a bit confusing to me at first, as Mama, Auntie, and Big Ma began talking to me about how I must do things in my life because I am of mixed heritage and a person of color. I must do the things they teach me, so I will not have problems in life, especially when I have my own family someday. They've also taught me that it's my responsibility to teach all the younger children in the family what I am learning. The younger children will do the same with the children that come after them. Everybody adheres to these rules in my family; it is known as the "safe way." It is important to know and pass down these guidelines to each new family member.

The safe way of doing things is knowing the lessons in life to protect myself and our family from harm and danger when we are away from home. No matter what we are doing outside the home, we must do it in a way that doesn't draw attention to ourselves. We must try to avoid asking anyone for help, if we can. That prevents interacting with others unnecessarily, which will prevent others from asking us questions. Our elders say that most of the time, when people ask us questions and don't like the answer we give them, it could cause critical situations that can affect our family's safety and life. It seems overly complicated to me. Ruthie says I think about it too much.

I have a wonderful family. I know my mama and daddy have some rough times. They are both very hotheaded, but they are good and caring people. They come from two diverse backgrounds, so they work hard to understand each other's perspective and approach to things. There is no doubt about the love they have for each other, the love for me and my sisters, and the love they have for our entire family. My parents do the best they can, and that makes me feel good. It works better for my sisters and me to stay with Big Ma and Papa. Ruthie, Baby Girl, and I do not question that decision; we accept it, and we love it. It is a wonderful life with our grandparents; they say it is the best thing for them too. Our talks are priceless, and we have learned so much from them.

One day, Papa told me himself why he did not have a home for a while. It was when he was a young man. Papa said that his mother was a special, sweet, and loving Muscogee Creek Nation lady named Golden Feather. Before any other people came to our land, before it was named America, it was called Turtle Island. My sisters and I learned that in Papa's family, there were nations, clans, and tribes. Papa says the word *tribe* really is the same word as *nation*, but the new people on the land changed the name nation to tribe. Papa says it's important that we remember that fact and be sure that our children know it as well.

Golden Feather was the niece of a clan chief named Brown Horse. Chief Brown Horse's nation, along with other nations, were helpful and kind for years and years to the colonists and others who followed, coming from Europe and England. The women of the clan taught the colonists how to farm, preserve foods, and make items for daily domestic life. The women also taught survival in and surrounding the home, when needed. The men in the clan taught the immigrants from across the waters how to hunt, fish, and make clothes and other items with skin and fur. The clan members also trained the new residents of the land in the skill of fighting and protecting their loved ones and property. Because Chief Brown Horse was a trader, he and the nation helped immigrants learn to build and sustain houses.

Our clan was prosperous, including Golden Feather. Golden Feather met one of the colonists and traders, a man name Clarence Leflore. Golden Feather and Mr. Leflore got along well, became friends, and eventually married. They had several houses on many acres of land. Big Ma says Papa told her that his parents were much better off financially than Big Ma and Papa will ever be. Papa said his parents shared with everyone. It did not matter who you were; if they could help, they would. Things went wonderfully for a long time. New people arrived in large numbers and settled into a new, thriving community. Everyone got along well, Papa said. Then, something happened—leaders representing the immigrants started having problems and were unhappy with several things. As soon as challenges appeared to be resolved with the immigrants, another issue of concern would be presented to the clan.

Papa said that one day, Great-Grandfather Clarence came home upset, and said that they might have to move someday. When Papa asked why, Great-Grandfather Clarence said that he thought that the new residents were trying to take over all the land. Papa said they had an advantage over our people because they had guns and other weaponry that the nation did not have. Papa said that my great-grandmother Golden Feather refused to believe that the new residents would do that. She thought all the new settlers had pure hearts, like her people and her husband.

Eventually, Grandmother Golden Feather's uncle, Chief Brown Horse, and many of the other nation members had to give up their lands to the settlers. The nations were told they must move on land where the new resident leaders wanted them to move, which was unfamiliar land and far away. The leaders also told Grandma Golden Feather's people that if they did not leave, they would not have their freedom any longer. Some of the young adults defied the new immigrant leaders and did not leave. They were taken away and put in confinement. Soon after, Grandfather Clarence moved Papa and Grandma Golden Feather off their land, before they were told to surrender it, to prevent future problems. The new house and land that his family moved to was nice, Papa said. It was a big, beautiful house on more acres than they'd had previously. At first, it was a little too fancy for Grandma Golden

Feather. She was partial to the first home, with so many memories, especially of her clan and nation. With her special touches to the house and land, however, Grandma Golden Feather turned the new house into a warm, nurturing home.

Papa's father hired a couple, James and Annette Redding, who lived on the land, to help them. Grandfather Clarence built a nice new house for Mr. and Mrs. Redding, with a big porch too. The Reddings had moved from Pennsylvania; they had three children—two girls and one boy, the youngest. Papa said they all lived together on the land and were family, helping each other and loving each other in the way our Creator instructs us to do.

Grandma Golden Feather was happy again, even though she missed her clan and nation. Not knowing where her people were and how they were doing made her cry often, Papa said. The only information that they knew about Grandmother Golden Feather's family was that they were going to a land called Oklahoma and that it was a long way to travel. Papa and his parents gave them plenty of food and blankets for the journey ahead of them. Grandfather Clarence promised Papa and Grandma Golden Feather that he would take them to visit their loved ones any time they wanted, after the clan and nation got settled in Oklahoma.

Family Nuggets and Sorrow

Sadly, those visits never happened. Grandfather Clarence became ill with a growth in his body in the fifth winter on the new land, and just before spring, he transitioned into the other life. Papa said it was a peaceful death. Grandfather Clarence wanted to be in the big living room around everyone for the last three months. Papa and Mr. Redding bought a huge bed, and Grandma Golden Feather put lots of pillows and blankets on it, just the way her husband liked it. Grandma Golden Feather was skilled in herbal medicine, like my Big Ma, so there was no pain for Grandfather Clarence. Papa said that during the last weeks his father was alive, they all spent the days reminiscing, laughing, singing, and making everything as enjoyable as possible for my great-grandfather Clarence. Papa said his father gave him advice on how Papa should do things after his father was gone, but Papa never spoke of these things in front of Grandma Golden Feather.

Grandfather Clarence was very respected and loved by the church, business friends, and town officials. Grandma Golden Feather allowed in all who wanted to visit Great-Grandfather Clarence because he was much beloved, and he loved the visits. The visiting lasted a month or so, but after that, it was just Grandma Golden Feather, Papa, and the Redding family who were present. Every day, Grandfather Clarence grew weaker and weaker, with continuous prayers and love surrounding him, until he transitioned into the Creator's arms. Grandma Golden Feather was grief-stricken and inconsolable for a long time. She lost so much weight from not eating that there was great concern from those closest to her.

Papa, the Redding family, and Grandpa Clarence's friends did everything they could to console Grandma Golden Feather. Finally, there was a turn around after friends asked Grandma Golden Feather to make a few quilts to sell in their town store. Papa was so happy because it helped his mother a great deal. The friends with the town store were friends with my great-grandparents. The time she spent with them reminded her of Grandfather Clarence, and on each return from her visit with them, she was better.

In just a short time, Grandma Golden Feather received new orders for quilts, and it kept her very busy. Eventually, Grandma Golden Feather went on with life again, without my great-grandfather. Every night after Papa's father died, Grandmother Golden Feather would leave a lit candle in her bedroom window. When Papa asked her why she put the candle in the window, Grandmother Golden Feather said she wanted Grandfather Clarence to be able to see in the dark room when he and our Creator came to get her, and they would be together again.

Before Grandfather Clarence became ill, he had spent years teaching Papa about being a person with good character and how to take care of everything. Papa says everything he knows is because of his parents, especially about being proud of who he is, where he came from, and what he could achieve in life. Papa learned how to be loving and caring to his family, how to handle money, and how to make smart business decisions. He also was taught how to be five to ten steps ahead in everything, so that he would not get caught off guard by unexpected situations in life.

We are a people who must be strong and not be affected by what other people say and do to us, Papa says. His parents embedded that in him. We need to know that our God and Creator, in every circumstance, will never leave us or abandon us. We must always keep this fact cemented in our hearts and minds throughout our lives. Papa says this is the most important fact of our lives—to know God, our Creator, is a solid foundation for us to stand on. We must know we are victorious, no matter what others think of us and no matter how they treat us.

The experiences we have with people who have issues against us, however, will have a negative impact on us at times. These experiences affect us so negatively that they might knock us down but only temporarily—we always get back on our feet. We are a people who will never give up, despite what others think, until the day we each transition from this life to the other life. When we transition to the other life, we will be reunited with all our loved ones and ancestors who transitioned before us.

All these nuggets of confidence are in each of us. These nuggets of confidence are given to us by God, our Creator. These nuggets of confidence are given to us through our elders. Our ancestors place these nuggets strategically in us with a plan for success, and they are priceless. No one can take these nuggets from us. Those who do not realize who we are and the great value we have only deceive themselves, Papa says.

By keeping blinders over their eyes and concrete slabs in front of the doors of their understanding, individuals who are not like us will deceive themselves into thinking that they are more than us and not equal, the way our God created us. Now I understand the importance of the flow of love, wisdom, and vital information from our Creator on how our people can survive in this life. All these key tools flow from God, through all our elders and ancestors who teach us how to use these tools. This priceless flow is the cement that makes us such special people and has enabled us to overcome great challenges over hundreds of years.

Two years and three weeks after Grandfather Clarence transitioned, Grandma Golden Feather, with her lit candle in her bedroom window, transitioned from this life to her eternal home with her Creator and Grandfather Clarence. Papa shed tears when he shared this part of our history. Papa said that he was so shocked and surprised when his mother did not wake up that morning. He never thought that he would not be able to spend more quality time with his mother and tell her all the things he wanted her to know. He could not accept the fact that he did not have the long goodbye, as he did with his father. Papa was angry because he was so busy that he missed time he could have spent with Grandma Golden Feather. Papa felt he had worked so hard to make Grandma Golden Feather's life happy, safe, and comfortable for the rest of her life, and now she was gone. Grief-stricken, Papa's directions that Grandfather Clarence had given him became nothing but a fog. He acted on only what he felt at the time. If it had not been for the Redding family, Papa said he would not have made it.

The Redding family was a great comfort to Papa. Just as he was pulling himself together, the community leaders came out to speak with him. Papa was told that the community needed the land that his parents had left him. Papa was also told that he would be reimbursed for the property but not for the full amount, and he had to leave within one year. Expansion of the town was taking place everywhere. Papa remembered what his father had said—that the new residents were taking over. The settlers had learned all there was to learn about the land. Papa's clans and nations and other kind nations had taught the new community members everything. They could survive on their own now, and this was what they did to our people. Papa felt like he could not make it each day. There was not anyone left in the world for him, except the Redding family; they were God's angels, assigned to love, guide, and hold Papa up.

Grandfather Clarence had known he could trust Mr. Redding. Grandfather Clarence had Mr. Redding's name, along with Papa's name, on all the legal documents, in case the immigrant leaders did not have Papa's best interest at heart. Papa said there was a giant void in his life, but he was feeling a bit stronger in day-to-day life. It was shortly after Papa was feeling like this that the new community leaders informed Papa of a change in the order—in six months, not twelve months, he would have to give up the land that his parents had left him. This was too much to bear. Losing his father and mother, Chief Brown Horse, the clan and the nation, and now to have to let go of his family home made Papa break.

There was a big dispute about this situation within the community. Many of the community members felt that, with all the family had done to build and help the community thrive, Papa deserved to keep his land. Some members of the community felt that Papa's loss was great, especially after all his demanding work in the community since Grandfather Clarence transitioned. Though many members were against the encroachment of Papa's land, the town officials made the decision that Papa still had only six months to cede the home and land. This destroyed Papa.

Big Ma, Papa, and Auntie taught us that as people, we are all the same. We are to treat everyone good and fair. My sisters, cousins, and I were taught that there are no differences in each other; that we are all the Creator's children, and we are all loved by Him. When Papa and Big Mama talked to us about Papa's situation when he was younger, my sisters and I learned a lot about where we come from, like I did when I found out about my dear African grandfather and African relatives.

When we see someone, we see a person. We never think anything about it if that person looks different from us. We never have thoughts about some family members looking different from each other, while other families might all look alike. My sisters, cousins, and I never were taught to see color in people. To the young folks in our family, color is merely descriptive of things, not people.

When I tell Baby Girl a story or when we play pretend, color is used to explain the sparkling blue water down by the waterfall and the pond, the pink ribbon in Mama's hair, the bright yellow sun in the sky, the brown porch, or the green grass. We were never taught to connect color with people, with human beings, with people who have spirits, souls, and bodies. Color was never in the same sentence when we were taught of a man and a woman, children and adults. We were only told that all people have a heart and feelings and are loved and love; color was never associated with it. We thought that everyone was different because the Creator uniquely made us all that way, and that was one of the main reasons that we were taught to love one another. We were taught and brought up that we are brothers and sisters from all lands, with all our differences, purposely made, and in one family—the family of God, our Creator. It was such a surprise when we found out that all families do not think this way. We thought all families didn't care, like we didn't, if you had different skin tones, features, cheekbones, and textures of hair.

It was surprising when our elders told us that everyone did not have that perspective in their families. There never was any emphasis put on us, as children growing up, about our color. There was never any emphasis put on us about others and their color. My daddy never told me, "My father is black, and my mother is French," nor did my mother say, "My mother is from the Senoia nation, and my father is Irish."

Papa did not tell us until now that his father, Grandfather Clarence, was a white man from England. We knew Grandma Golden Feather's mother was of the Muscogee Creek Nation, and we just found out that her father was the grandson of a black slave, who was separated from his parents at an early age because of the rules of slavery. Grandmother Golden Feather said she never knew about her father's people because knowledge of the lineage was cut off and because her father did not allow them to talk about it. Grandmother Golden Feather did say that her father taught them African words, and she shared those words with Papa, and he shared them with us. Mama, Daddy, Papa, and Big Ma always spoke to us in English. English is the primary language of this land now, so it is our language because we were born here, and this is our land.

When I was very little, Mama and Daddy once told Ruthie and me, when Baby Girl was born, that they were shield-keepers for us, and their job was to keep a shield around us while we were with them in this land we live in. Our parents told us that one day, when we got older, we would be shield-keepers too.

I don't know about Ruthie, but I am beginning to understand what they mean by saying that when we are at a certain age, they don't want us to ask questions. That's because they don't want us to know some things too soon because that could rob us of our innocence and tamper with our loving and pure thoughts. With all this information that our elders want us to know, I see things this way: I see there is a huge invisible door on the end of this property, facing the road. The road leads to the outside world, which is the entirety of Turtle Island—or, as it has been renamed, America. Our elders kept their shields up and only opened the door to the outside world a little at a time and only as we developed and matured. The door is not completely open for us to see everything—not yet. Our elders are starting to share some valuable information they want us to know now, so that we have a greater understanding of why we do what we do and say what we say.

CHAPTER 3

Dismal Truths

———————⟫◆⟪———————

T he information that we have learned takes us back to our
dear Papa and how the new community leaders were
able to enforce encroachment on his land. Most of my
unanswered questions were answered when Papa's ordeals in
life were revealed to me. Papa was told that because he had black
blood in him, he was not qualified to continue to live on the
land that Grandfather Clarence had bought and made beautiful.
Papa had to give up his home because of the "one-drop statute."
It did not matter that his mother was Golden Feather, a royal
member of the Muscogee Nation and directly related to Chief
Brown Horse's clan. They are the original people who lived on
this land for centuries before the arrival of immigrants. It did not
matter that her father was a black man who came from a family
of people who lived on this land before others arrived. It did not
matter that Papa's African ancestors were violently forced from
their homeland, to travel the oceans for months, to live in a place
where they worked for others who prospered and not themselves.

It did not matter that the one-drop-of-blood theory that they
speak of so negatively relates to the people who built this land
that we live on, with no payment or benefits given to them. It
did not matter that Papa's father was a white European trader,
settler, community leader, and a good man. He was a man who

was intelligent enough to know that all people are the same, and no one is inferior to the other. It made no difference that Papa had an education and helped his father build the very community from they were expelling him. It meant nothing to the immigrant leaders that Papa, as a young, prominent businessperson in his community, helped people have a better life and showed them how to sustain that life. None of the time or money he put into the community mattered when it came down to the decision to encroach on Papa's property.

Papa has Negro blood in him, which make him a Negro man. He was not looked at as a decent American citizen but as a Negro man who had no rights. They wanted the prime piece of land, and they got it. Papa could have rebelled and fought to keep his land, but he knew that his freedom was at risk and that the immigrant leaders would burn down the beautiful land and all that was on it, rather than let Papa have it.

The one-drop-of-blood law was unfair, but Grandfather Clarence had seen the unfairness and had prepared for his son ahead of time' he'd prepared for these types of situations. Papa stayed close to the Redding family. Still financially well off, Papa went up toward the mountains and bought more land. Papa and Mr. Redding built two houses on the property, and Papa made sure they were safe and secure. This time, the Reddings lived in the main house, with a porch built exactly like the porch Grandfather Clarence had built for the Redding family years before. Mr. Redding and Papa built two additional pillars on the extra-large porch and painted them gold, in honor of Grandfather Clarence and Grandma Golden Feather. Papa instructed Mr. Redding to rent out the second house whenever he wanted, that there was no need to rush at all.

Because his loss was so massive, however, my dear Papa's spirit was broken. He did not want to stay near the area where he had been for all his life. He felt as though he no longer had a home. It was too great a test for him, personally, and he did not want to do anything to let down his Creator, his parents, and all his ancestors who had come before him. Papa had been taught, by his parents and through generations of his people, to love and obey his Creator, to have dignity, and to be proud of who he was and where he came from. Papa did what he was taught—walk in love throughout his life, despite any situations and persecutions he experienced in his life. Papa felt strongly that there were too many memories for him, and he made Mr. Redding steward over most of what Papa owned and over his affairs.

Papa left, wanting to get far away from the town his beloved parents helped to build, and he set out for Oklahoma to build a life with his great-uncle, Chief Brown Horse, and the rest of the nation family. When he reached his destination, he found only eleven cousins to greet him. Papa's relatives told him of the perilous journey that his loved ones had gone through. Great-Uncle Chief Brown Horse and most of Papa's family had died, along with thousands of the Creek Nation, as they traveled to Oklahoma. Papa's people were not the only ones to feel the wrath of the elements, walking on this more than five-thousand-mile journey. Thousands and thousands of Cherokee, Seminole, Chickasaw, Choctaw, among other nations, died as well. It was a cold, cruel, and heartless journey, with unbearable suffering taking place. It was too much for any human being. There were cases of starvation, exposure, dysentery, cholera, whooping cough, and mental collapse. All these diseases and other illnesses attacked the people mercilessly. Papa said that the deadly journey was eventually called the Trail of Tears. A large memorial was created afterward, there in Oklahoma, for all those who lost their lives and were affected by this tragedy. Papa was told it took three years to build the memorial. It was surrounded by beautiful gardens and artifacts made with gorgeous stones.

Standing in front of the memorial, Papa was able to pay tribute to those he loved and missed. Love, grief, and sadness poured out of Papa's heart toward all the people he lost. He expressed gratefulness and appreciation to his parents, to all his ancestors, to his great-uncle Chief Brown Horse, the clan, and the nation. He thanked them all for what they had had done for his mother, father, and him, especially in teaching him so much when he was a little boy. For the first time, he felt the presence of both his parents and was finally able to accept his mother, Golden Feather's, death. To honor both his parents, Papa rededicated his life to them by promising to do all they taught him and to pass it on for generations, if he ever had children.

Standing at that memorial, Papa started a new life by rededicating his life to God, asking God, the Creator, to forgive him of his anger and disobedience during this trying time in his life. By forgiving all those who had hurt him and his parents, Papa felt renewed. He thanked his parents for being present with him at the memorial, and he knew within his spirit that they would be with him constantly, within his heart. Papa longed for the days at home with his parents but was comforted by knowing they would all be together again on the day he transitioned from this life.

Papa stayed at the memorial for three days, until his cousins finally convinced him to come with them to eat and get much-needed sleep. Papa said he was so exhausted that he slept and stayed in bed for a week. He only got out the bed when necessary and to eat sometimes. Papa and his cousins experienced all types of emotions and feelings, spending many days sharing different memories. Papa stayed several months with his family in Oklahoma, trying to make it his new home. After quality time with his Creator and his family, Papa knew it was time to leave. Papa's family did not want him to leave and assured him of the love and support he would need to a make Oklahoma his permanent home. Papa was grateful for the healing he had received there in Oklahoma, but he did not get a confirmation within his spirit to call it home.

Home? Papa realized he had a home, a home that existed now only in his heart and mind. Papa felt that he would never have a home again and that he would never smile again. He realized that, in life, you can have all the money needed to reach financial goals, but if you do not have the ones you love in your life, it means nothing. Papa told his cousins he was a traveler now—that was his life. All his relatives whom he had loved dearly and was close to were not on the land, physically, anymore. All his loved ones were gone. Papa said that he would just cherish his memories, knowing that they were with him in spirit, as he continued his life.

Reaping and the Covering

Papa decided to be a tradesman, like his father, Grandfather Clarence, was before he married Golden Feather. Papa traveled the world and used all the knowledge and tools he learned from his father and his uncle Chief Brown Horse. For years, there was still an emptiness inside of him, even though his life was full of activity, but it was nothing like what he grew up with. As Papa traveled, his wealth grew, as did his skills and knowledge. Mr. Redding and his family were loyal to Papa, and Papa would visit them at least twice a year. Mr. Redding would invest Papa's money in land and other investments that brought back good returns and continued to increase Papa's wealth. Mr. Redding looked after Papa's affairs like Papa was his own son. The relationship was a loving and trusted one between Papa and the Redding family. They were not people of color, and they were good to Papa. Papa wished that everyone had hearts like them.

On one of Papa's visits home, he went to church with the Reddings, as he usually did. That was when he saw Big Ma singing in the choir. Mrs. Redding invited Big Ma to dinner the next week. Big Ma was very shy, but her family gave her permission, and she accepted. Big Ma's family had a chaperone from her family attend all of her and Papa's time together. The rest is history!

The emptiness in Papa's life was not there when he was around Big Ma. Papa never traveled again. He built a house on one of his properties that Mr. Redding had bought for him and made it a home for him and Big Ma. Papa and Big Ma married a year after meeting each other. Both Papa and Big Ma said they knew God was giving them a chance to have a family so they could change the way things are in life because of our color.

Papa says that it's his goal to make our lives better so that we will not have to go through what they and our other ancestors have gone through. So here they are, all these years later, at the same family house, changing our lives for the better.

Mr. and Mrs. Redding are much older now and still live in the same house that Papa built for them years ago. Papa gave the Reddings the house and all the land on the property, as well as other properties, in appreciation for Mr. Redding's honesty and good stewardship over all Papa had for so many years.

Papa hired a family name the Carters to live in the rental house on Mr. Redding's property. The Carters look after Mr. and Mrs. Redding and the property. The Carters have three children—two boys and a baby girl. The Carters are wonderful people who care for the Reddings, just like the Reddings cared for Papa and his parents so well. Papa and Big Ma's house is just up the road from the Reddings' house, so they—and all of us—can love on the Reddings and watch over them too. They are such sweet, good people. Papa reminds us that the Reddings are angels who God, the Creator, sent to Papa's life to be the family that Papa needed. That is true, and they are also my family too. It seems to me that family is a matter of the heart and blood, and sometimes, family are assigned to us, given by God, our Creator. Both types of families are matters of the heart and of the spirit.

One of the greatest revelations for me and Ruthie from my family's talk about color was the that, for many reasons, some individuals do not like people of color. I am so thankful that the Redding family never looked at Papa and saw color. It is hard to understand that concept, but it is real, my family says. It is so real that my family keeps those family safety rules constantly before us.

We must each obey the rules when we are away from home. It does not matter what age we are; we must follow the family safety rules. We are told to handle situations a certain way when away from home. We are to avoid conversations if we see anyone who might have an issue with us. If people have a problem with us—if we are confronted in any way, whether positive or negative—we are to cooperate with them and submit to them, within reason. We will be intentional in not agitating them. We are not to get into a disagreement with them, act angry, or raise our voices. We are to say "yes, sir" or "yes ma'am" and do our utmost to neutralize the situation as quickly as possible. We must do this, our elders tell us, so that we will have a more positive outcome and will make it back home.

Because Mama has shared with me about my daddy's father's experience of being a slave, and Papa has shared with all of us about his experiences in life being biracial, I must trust them and know they have my best interest at heart. I know they want the best for me. I will try my best to be obedient, and I am urging Ruthie, Baby Girl, and all my cousins to do the same. We don't have issues at the schoolhouse—we are all colored there, or, as I like to say now, we are all the exotic blend.

I understand that things better, and I thank my Creator for giving us smart elders and ancestors, who have taught us how to survive in this life. We know what to do if we run into any situations because of our color. After doing all that our elders say, we can only trust God that things will turn out so that we will not be harmed.

The Sealing of the Covering

It is Saturday. I am sitting on the porch in Big Ma's rocking chair. I am enjoying the peace and tranquility that comes with a day like this. Papa is in his rocking chair, enjoying the splendor as well. He begins to play his flute; I always enjoy hearing it.

It's been months since Papa opened and shared from his heart about some of his life experiences. Papa says all the time, "Never give up."

I decide to ask Papa something, so I say, "Papa, with all the heartbreaks, all the anger, and all the loneliness, how did you not give up? How did you keep going?"

Papa looks at me and smiles. "I have been waiting for you to ask me that. Now I know you are almost an adult."

Surprised, I say, "How did you know I was going to ask, Papa?"

"My father and mother prepared me for this life in the best way they knew how. They were not perfect people—no one is, and no one will ever be. They made mistakes, and, Peaches, they learned from those mistakes. My parents shared things with me about their mistakes and the things they did right—when they thought I was ready to hear it. I thought I understood a lot of things they taught me, but I really didn't understand until I went through tough times. They told me specific things to remember, and they were extremely helpful in life, but I learned the greatest things from my parents by watching them. I hope you will be able to say the same about me and Big Ma."

Papa looks straight up at the sky without saying anything. His face looks like he's seeing someone he hasn't seen in a long time, someone he loved. Papa picks up his flute again and plays "Engraved in His Palm." I want to ask him something about what he just said, but I can't. It's like something sacred is happening at this moment, and all I need to do is just be still and be quiet.

Papa continues to play the flute, looking intently up to the sky. His face is glowing now, and his expression shows reverence, honor, and devotion. I know, at this very moment, that Papa is experiencing an extremely spiritual visitation from the Creator and his parents. Papa is receiving specific anointed instructions from his royal visitors regarding me. Whatever is happening right now, it enables me to see beauty in the sky that I have never seen before. I feel nature alive, all around me, and new sensations. Every moment is so beautiful. Everything is magnified—the warmth of the sun on my body, and the fragrance of the flowers, and the sound of the birds singing, and the wind blowing through tall, gorgeous trees.

The sound of Papa's sweet flute assists this ecstasy. This ecstasy is orchestrated by the noise of many waters, which, as my siblings and I have been taught from the Bible, is what our

Creator's voice is like. I realize I'm moving, floating through the air. I am lying down on a beautiful bright rug—a rug braided with love, joy, and understanding. I am covered from my neck down to my feet with a blanket that is visually glistening with a mixture of all colors. This blanket is exquisite, and it has been created with a heavenly fabric called peace, which radiates downward. This blanket is breathtaking, and as it radiates downward into my body, all the elements of the blanket are welded into the core of my existence.

I do not have words in my vocabulary to describe what I am changed into right now in this present state, nor to describe what I feel. Tranquility would only be the seed for this state. Where I am right now is the perfect place for me. I could stay right in this place forever. I wouldn't have to concern myself for the rest of my life with trying not to upset those who don't like who I am because of my color. I could get used to this—no fear or concerns of my being harmed or of loved ones being harmed or cheated because of our heritage. It would be wonderful if I did not have to worry about my family, and we could all live in this security, understanding, and acceptance mode that I am experiencing right now at this moment. If my Creator lets me stay here, it would be simply fine with me. I would not mind at all.

Oh, wait—what about Mama and Daddy? Who would look out for Baby Girl? Ruthie is too impatient with Baby Girl. And how would Big Ma, Papa, and Arlee get all those chores done without my help? My family needs me, so I cannot be selfish. I won't think on those things right now. I am just going to enjoy this splendid feeling and God's exquisite creations that I am able to see and experience in these moments. How I wish all my loved ones could experience this feeling of relief and comfort. I am loved and safe, with no worries or cares. I will just bask in this peacefulness and world of fulfillment. Thank you, God, for manifesting Yourself to me. Thank you, God, for the vessel You choose to use to accomplish Your manifestations. Thank you, Papa, for obeying God and ushering me into His presence.

"Peaches, Peaches, wake up, Peaches. It's time to set the dinner table. Come on, now. Wake up and wash your hands. Aren't you hungry, baby?"

I can hear Mama calling my name, but it's so hard to open my eyes.

"Peaches, do you hear me?"

I look over my right shoulder and see Mama standing behind the screen door. The door is open but not too much, keeping the flies from coming in.

"You awake now?" Mama asks.

"Yes, Mama, I'm awake. I'm coming." I sound sleepy. I can't understand why I slept so hard, though. I still feel like I could go to bed and sleep all night. As I stand up, a piece of writing paper falls off my lap. I pick up the paper and recognize the cream-colored paper and Papa's handwriting. I start reading the note:

> To Peaches. The answer to your questions,
> how did I not give up? How did I keep going?

I remember the talk that Papa and I start to have about not giving up and how to keep on going. I remember Papa playing his flute. Wait a minute—I remember. I remember the sky. I remember the braided rug. I remember my cover of peace. I remember everything! I know Mama is waiting on me, but I realize that I have had a special spiritual experience. I have to read what this note says now:

> Answer:
> God, our Creator, wants the island to listen.
> God, our Creator, wants the nations to listen.
> God, our Creator, will never leave you or give up
> on you and will never abandon you.
> Trust God, the Creator, with all your heart.
> Don't listen to your negative thoughts or to other
> people's negative thoughts.

God, our Creator, will guide your steps every day
of your life because He will be a lamp to your feet,
and He will be a light to any path you are on.
God, our Creator, will not lie to you. He can't. He
is not a man.
With God, our Creator, all things are possible.
God, our Creator, will strengthen you, and He will
protect you from the evil one.
Lastly, Peaches:

> Can a mother forget the baby at her breast and
> have no compassion on the child she has borne?
> Though she may forget, I will not forget you!
> See, I have engraved you on the palms of my
> hands; your walls are ever before me. (Isaiah
> 49:15–16 NIV)

I love you, Peaches.
Your Papa

I just stand there, looking at the note. I read it two more times and start to read it a third time when Mama calls me again.

"Coming, Mama," I say as I walk through the front door.

Mama peeks out of the kitchen, looking at me as I enter the house. "I see you have the note that Papa left you. Put it away in a special place so you can always keep it. You will need it someday."

"Yes, Mama. Where is my Papa?"

"Papa and Big Ma went to town earlier. They should be back before dark."

I'm a little disappointed. I want to thank Papa for taking the time to write a note after I fell asleep in the middle of our time together. I run to my room and fold my note neatly. Then I stick it into my velvet-and-satin keepsake box that Big Ma made me for Christmas. Yep, this is right where it belongs, with all my other precious belongings.

MH (Mental Health) A state of well being mentally and all it encompasses.

MHC (Mental Health Condition) A illness that affects and individual's thinking, feelings, mood, and behavior.

MHC Trigger: Colleen and all her family have to live daily with cultural pressure and stress of survival. They have to live with and maintain "the rules to safely make it back home," every moment of the day that an individual is away from home.

MHC Trigger: The intimidation and prejudice experienced by Papa Norris when the one-drop statute was applied to him and other multiracial individuals. The negative treatment of people of color by those who felt they were superior to them.

MHC Trigger: The fear and uncertainty of Golden Feather and her Muscogee family and all the Native American clans and nations who traveled on the Trail of Tears. The grief and loss over the thousands of people that died on the Trail of Tears. The trauma and the effect it had on all the loved ones at that time and the generations that followed.

MHC Trigger: The injustice in the taking Papa Norris's property. The threat of destruction of the property if not surrendered.

MHC Trigger: Papa Norris's grief and loss over the death of his parents and the lack of freedom in being able to have prosperity openly.

Scriptural Support:

So, it shall be, when your son asks you in time to come, saying, what is this? That you shall say to him by strength of hand the Lord brought us out of Egypt, out of the house of bondage. (Exodus 13:14 NKJV)

Blessed be the God and Father of our Lord Jesus Christ, the Father of mercies and God of all comfort, who comforts us in all our tribulations, so that we may be able to comfort those who are in any trouble, with the comfort that we ourselves are comforted by God. (2 Corinthians 1:3–5 NKJV)

CHAPTER 4

Bridge Crossing

———————————

I am trying to concentrate as I sit at my desk at the schoolhouse. It's difficult because of the heat, humidity, and my growling, hungry stomach. My bothersome classmate Wilford, who is sitting straight across from me, isn't making things any better.

"Eighteen. What's the answer to eighteen?" Wilford whispers to me.

"Virginia," I whisper back, with my head still bowed toward the paper on my desk. Just my eyes are turned toward Wilford. I don't mind helping him. I will help whoever I can at school because it is difficult. Wilford is an exception; he cannot get to school all the time because his mom is sick, so he stays home sometimes to help take care of her. If I don't get caught and don't get in trouble, I will help when needed.

I like Wilford—he is fun to be around—but in class, he cuts up too much. He does not act like he is seventeen, the same age as me and Cousin Arlee, but we are more mature than he is. When the test is over and all are turned in, I look at Arlee in the next row, three seats back. I give her the "we out of here for the weekend" look, and she grins back.

I am so lucky that Arlee and I get to attend the same school. They opened the new schoolhouse for high school, and it's between my house and Arlee's house. It is so convenient for us. Sometimes, I stay at her house, but most of the time, she stays with us at home, with Big Ma and Papa. We have one year before we complete high school, and we have our plans for the future. Arlee wants to become a nurse, get married, and have children. I want to become a seamstress, a wife, and a mother. I want to make my own clothes and sell them. I am going to open a shop and sell my clothes across the country. Then, I will get married and have children. I want to have a lot of children and grandchildren, and I want them to spend fun times at my house, like I do with Big Ma—nothing but peace, laughter, and happiness. My children can help me with my clothing business. That is the life I want, and everything will be perfect because we can all be involved, and we will always be together.

I love children, and I miss taking care of Baby Girl like I did when she was small, even though I am still her second mama. She says that wherever I go in life, she is going with me, and that is fine with me. I will get an understanding with my future husband that Baby Girl stays with me; it is a package deal.

Wilford slips me a note before we are dismissed, and I stick it in my pocket quickly, before the teacher sees it. Standing outside the school after class, Arlee and I talk to some of our friends before we head home for the weekend. I reach in my pocket for the note from Wilburn. Arlee looks over my shoulder so she can read it. The note is a reminder about the community picnic that is taking place tomorrow. Mama said Arlee and I can go.

I'm not I really interested in going; I'd rather stay home and have nice relaxing day. Arlee wants to go, but she won't go if I don't. A friend that Arlee likes, Jacob, will be there. I guess I will go so at least one of us will have fun. We'll have to prepare something to take to contribute to the menu. Big Ma will have some ideas. Maybe Mama will let Ruthie go with us. It'll be good for her to get out too.

After arriving home, Big Ma says she will make baked beans and deviled eggs; Ruthie and I will make fried chicken. Papa is contributing a big jug of his sun tea, and I am starting to look forward to our picnic.

Arlee, Ruthie, and I are in the bedroom, later in the evening, trying new styles with our hair up. We all get too hot with it down. Ruthie is going with us, and Baby Girl is pouting because she is too young to go. Papa will drop us off at the picnic, and Auntie and her boyfriend, Joseph, will pick us up. If I wasn't going, I could just sleep in tomorrow; it's been a long week. Oh well, it will be fun for the girls, so I might as well get over it. Some our friends from church will be there, so it won't be too bad.

Mama and Auntie arrive early on Saturday morning for the weekend; Joseph brings them now. Joseph and Auntie spend a lot of time together. He's becoming like part of the family. He spends a lot of time with Papa too, when he is here. Auntie and Mama have cookies and brownies to add to our picnic treats. Now, I'm a little excited to go, just for those special sweets.

Before we know it, we are in the carriage and on our way. Arlee and Ruthie are riding inside, and I am riding up top, next to Papa. It seems like just yesterday that I was too small to ride next to Papa. Now I can even drive the carriage myself—Papa taught me how. The picnic baskets, blankets, and pillows are all on the seat behind me and Papa, tied down so they won't fall off.

When we arrive, I recognize many people who are socializing and seem to be having an enjoyable time already. Papa and I are trying to find a good spot for us, when all of a sudden, I see Wilbur approaching us with a big smile. He has his girlfriend, Ruby, with him, and she has a welcome smile on her face. Ruby and I have known each other since we were little girls in Sunday school and in the teen art club at the library.

"So, you made it!" Ruby greets us with a happy tone.

"We've been keeping an eye out for you," Wilford says in an even happier tone than Ruby. "We have a large space for all of you, right over there near us."

As Papa gets all our picnic gear down, Wilbur takes the blankets and pillows out of Papa's hands.

"I will take care of this for you, sir," Wilford says respectfully.

"We have it all, Mr. Norris. My brother is going to help. Here he comes now."

A young man walks up and relieves me, Ruthie, and Arlee of everything in our hands—the baskets, the jug of sun tea, and the books and magazines we brought to read.

"Sir, this is my brother Lander. Lander Banks," Wilford says.

"Well hello, son. Nice to meet you. Haven't I seen you somewhere in town? Can't place where, though," Papa says.

Wilford's brother looks Papa straight in the eye. "Probably at the post office, sir. I deliver mail for the county."

Papa nods in confirmation. "That's right. You deliver on that—what you call it? Uh, motorbike—that motorbike. This is my granddaughter Ruthie, my niece Arlee, and this young lady is my oldest grandchild, Colleen."

Papa introduced us with such pride. I hope we live up to all his expectations of us. I was embarrassed when he introduced me. I don't know why; I just feel strange. I'm nervous.

"Pleasure to meet all of you," this Lander person says, his arms filled with our picnic gear. The funny thing is, the entire time he was speaking, he was looking at me, and the awkwardness of the moment feels overwhelming.

I quickly give Papa a kiss on the cheek, saying, "See you later, Papa." I reach for Ruthie's arm, then Arlee's arm, and started walking between the two, toward Ruby and Wilford, saying cheerfully, "Lead the way."

Ruby walks us over to the area they have chosen for us. The location is perfect. Every place that Ruthie and Arlee could go is within my view. It's a spot that's cornered off away from the crowd by pink and white floral shrubbery. The large grassy area has picnic tables and places by the stream where you can sit. In separate locations are an assortment of trees with blossoms on them, and a tire swing on each tree.

"What a wonderful place this is," Ruthie says to me, grinning.

I love to see Ruthie happy. She can seem a little different to some people, but our family understands her. Ruthie does not like anything unpleasant in her life. She wants things to always go her way or she is unhappy. Mama, Big Ma, and Papa have told her many times that life does not work that way. They've told her that she needs to change her way of thinking, and she will be much happier.

It is simply good to see her smiling and talking to others and not so into herself. Wilford, Ruby, and Lander are so kind. In a flash, we have everything set up for our picnic spot. Our picnic blanket is on the ground, just a hand's throw from the stream. I sit here, enjoying the scenery and alone time, while Ruthie and Arlee are being social butterflies.

Arlee's friend has not arrived yet. I hope he makes it; she will be disappointed if he does not. Ruby and Wilford are helping other people set up. They have such servants' hearts. *I should go help them*, I think. *No, I am going to spoil myself today.* I decide to get my book out and read. I can never read at home. There is always something to do to help Big Ma and Papa. I don't mind, though; they have done so much for our family.

I look up from my book and see Lander coming. Why do I get nervous when I look at him? I look back down at my book before he gets close enough to see me. I really want to keep on looking at him. I like the way he walks—with confidence, like an important leader. My heart is beating fast. Oh, he must be almost to the blanket.

"Hi, Ms. Colleen. Are you enjoying yourself?" Landon says in a deep but gentle voice.

I look up at him. "I am enjoying myself. It's very relaxing here, especially at this spot."

"Do you mind company?" Lander asks, in a tone like he really hopes I will say yes.

I think, *Okay, I'll find out what kind of guy he is.* Now that I see him up close up, he is very handsome—beautiful skin, black shiny hair, clean-cut nails, a neatly cut moustache. His outfit and shoes are quite appropriate for a picnic. *Wow! He didn't look like this when we arrived.* I wonder if he is like the type Mama warns me about—a ladies' man who gets around a lot.

"No, I don't mind at all," I say, looking down at my book. "Have a seat."

I suddenly feel very inexperienced, shy, and unequipped to sit on a picnic blanket with this gorgeous guy who wants to be in my company. After he sits down, I realize he smells good too.

"Thank you, Ms. Colleen. Thank you very much," he says cheerfully. He sits next to me but not too close. "Wow, this is a great spot—a good place to unwind."

"Yes, it is," I say quietly, still not knowing what to say and feeling like a fish out of water. What do I say? I've talked to guys before. What is wrong with me today? What can I say? The silence is agonizing.

Just as I'm about to say something, he starts to say something, and we talk at the same time. We both look at each other and burst into laughter. The laughter breaks the awkwardness and cuts the tension away.

Lander looks me in the eyes and says, "You know, I am not very good at this."

"At what?" I don't have any idea of what he's talking about.

Lander has a boyish smile. "At striking up a conversation with a young lady, especially a beautiful lady like you. I work a lot, and that doesn't leave much time for socializing. I have a confession, Ms. Colleen."

A confession? I think. *We just met, and already he has said I'm beautiful and that he has a confession in the same breath. This is not starting off too good.* Putting my guard up instantly, I try to look at him with a tougher look than before. "What kind of confession?"

Lander moves so we are sitting face-to-face on the blanket. "Today isn't the first day I have seen you."

"It isn't?" I'm incredibly surprised and wonder what is going on with this guy.

"No. I see you arriving at the schoolhouse and going into the library at least three or four times a week. I have seen you since school started. Sometimes I see you in town with your grandparents on the weekend. I figured I better get my nerve up to talk to you before school gets out and you have summer vacation. You are the most exquisite lady I have ever seen, and I wanted to meet you."

"Have you been following me?" I ask, concerned that I might have a big problem on my hands.

"No, not at all. I would never disrespect you like that. As I told your grandfather, I work for the post office, and I have my daily runs at the same time you go to your classes and the library. Sometimes I work on the weekend, and that's when I see you in town. I just wanted to meet you and talk to you. I asked Wilford if he knew if you were coming today. I prayed that you would. I wanted to talk to you and ask if we could possibly spend time together. I really want to get to know you."

I don't know what to say; I'm speechless. Can this really be happening to me? Looking into his eyes, I want to see sincerity. Big Ma says that the eyes are the windows to our souls. I want to look into his eyes and see what I saw. I am shaking by this time; I am so nervous. I hope he doesn't see my head shaking—it does that sometimes when I am very nervous. I look into his eyes, just knowing I will see deceit and sneakiness, but as I look, I tell Lander, "I don't know what to say. I don't know what to think. I just don't know."

Lander looks at me with understanding and patience. "You don't have to say or do anything. Take as much time as you like and think about it. Is that possible—for you to think about it?"

I'm still looking into his eyes. I see no deceit, no sneakiness at all. Inside, I feel that he is a sincere and honest man. I look in his eyes a little deeper, and I see something else. I see hurt in his eyes, hurt and disappointment. When I see the hurt, I almost feel like I'm invading a private place. I quickly stop searching his eyes and say, "Yes, I will think about it. I will take some time to think about what you have asked."

"Well, thank you, Ms. Colleen, for your consideration. I appreciate your time." Lander stands up and appears to be leaving.

Surprised at his actions, I quickly ask, "Are you leaving already?"

"Well, yes, ma'am. I don't want to impose. I'm sure you have things in mind to do while picnicking today," Lander says politely.

Disappointed at the thought of him leaving, I say, "Lander, I would be pleased for you to stay, and we can enjoy this beautiful day together. How does that sound to you?"

"Now that sounds just fine, Ms. Colleen. That sounds just fine."

I'm relieved that he's not leaving, and I'm enjoying the picnic so much that I don't want it to end. To think that I did not want to come. I would have missed out on the first romantic day in my life! Ruthie and Arlee are enjoying themselves also. Arlee's friend Jacob did get here shortly after we arrived, and Ruthie was fluttering around with everyone she knew. We played games, enjoyed the food, laughed, and had a few contests too.

In the evening, I sit on one of the tire swings as Lander pushes me. We've had such an enjoyable time together. Lander is still pushing me on the swing when Auntie and Joseph arrive. When Auntie and I look at each other, we smile at once because we both know that we have a lot to talk about later.

Lander and Jacob help us get all our picnic gear together. As everyone walks ahead, Lander says to me, "Today was an incredible day for me; you know that?"

"I enjoyed myself as well, Lander. It was a good day for me too. It's the best time I have had in a long time."

"Thank you for allowing me to spend the day with you. You are the special lady that I knew you would be and more," Lander says.

I am so happy to hear that from Lander. I feel some type of connection with him. "I would like for us to spend more time together. I really would."

Lander breaks out in the biggest grin I have ever seen on a person's face. "That is great, Ms. Colleen, seeing as you are going to be my wife and all," Lander says with excitement.

"Wife! You're moving too fast," I tell him, laughing.

"You will see. I am going to make you so happy that you will never want us to be apart—ever."

By this time, we've reached Auntie and Joseph.

"Well, I guess this is goodbye for now. I will see you soon," Lander says.

"I have to talk to my folks about it, but I don't believe they will have a problem with it. You will have to come and meet my mother and grandmother, though." I smile at him.

"Yes, ma'am!" Lander says as he bows to me a little.

Oh, this guy is bowing to me too? I look at Auntie, and she winks at me, and we both giggle a little. I look back after we've ridden for a minute or so, and Lander is standing there in the same spot, watching us still. He hasn't moved, and he's watching me get farther and farther away. Lander waves two or three times.

I feel a little sad at leaving him. We laughed so much. I like him; he makes me feel good about everything. I do hope I see him again. How can I meet a person, and the same day, I am feeling I want him to be in my life? Just as a friend, though; just as a friend. He was very presumptuous with the wife comment. I'm not thinking about that! I have much to do before something like that happens in my life.

I look back. I still can see him far off, and then I can't see him anymore. He stayed there; I like him. It felt good that he wanted me in his sight until he could not see me anymore. Lander. Lander. I even like saying his name. He makes me feel incredibly special—special, indeed.

Lander and I have a nice summer! He is such a kind, gentle man. He says he is my protector, and I like that. He works extremely hard during the week, and we spend time together out at Big Ma and Papa's too. Sometime Wilford and Ruby come out. They all love it out here, and my grandparents do not mind the company. They say it keeps them young. Mama and Daddy are spending more time together out at the family house. Things are so much better now that Daddy does not work so hard. Daddy actually can be a very nice person, with a sense of humor. We would have never known that about Daddy if Mama had let him continue to work all those days each week. Daddy is a lot more demonstrative in showing affection to Mama and all the family. It's amazing what being overworked can do to a person. Auntie and Joseph spend a lot of time together at the family house. Papa and Big Ma's big, long porch is filled with friends and family now, and they love it. Lander loves to spend time here because he says he wants us to have a family like this someday—all together, enjoying each other.

Installing Deep Roots

Lander, Wilford, and their sister, Maria, have had a tough time in life, especially recently, when their mother, Mrs. Annette Banks, died. Mrs. Banks was a strong lady, Lander tells me. I never met her, but I could tell she was close to all her children by the way Lander talks about her. Lander says that his life was complicated because Mrs. Banks was white, and Mr. Banks is Negro. Lander's father is a traveling minister, and his mother was seamstress, like Big Ma. He does not have to say another word because I know of the heartache my elders have gone through in having a mixed marriage and children who are Negro. There are so many challenging situations we must go through, just to live a normal life.

People of color must be extraordinarily strong in this world. We must accept the hardships and cruelties that come our way because we are people of color. We must learn to bear the burdens, until the day comes when life will change for us. Lander's mother died a few months after he met Big Ma, Mama, and the rest of the family. He visited often, always on the weekend.

When Mrs. Banks was close to passing, Lander's employer allowed him to take time off to be with her and his siblings. I sent him letters to encourage him, as he stayed close by her, not leaving her side during that time. When his mother passed away, Lander drove out to the family house the next day and sat on the porch with me, Big Ma, and Papa all day. We had time alone, as Big Ma and Papa both would come and go off the porch, going about activities. Lander talked about his mother and how kind she was to Lander and to everybody. I allowed him to talk without interrupting him. Lander kept repeating that his mother needed the best care, that she deserved it, and he made sure she got it—the best medicine, a nurse to clean and care for her, and someone to keep the house and cook the meals.

"You made sure all that was taken care of?" I asked.

"Yes, ma'am. I work two jobs and made sure she was cared for like the queen she was. Maria and Wilford had a big part in that happening too," Lander said, as tears ran down his cheeks.

My heart broke for him. I took his hand and told him how proud I was to know a man like him. Lander said that's what his mother would say to him, over and over. It was a tough day for him, but I am glad he spent it with us. Papa and Lander walked around the land for an hour or so. Papa said some man-time would be good for him. I know Papa was a help for Lander, seeing as Papa had such a tough time when his mother, Golden Feather, passed away suddenly, so many years ago.

Lander asked if I would come to his mother's service. I did not have to search deep into his eyes to see the hurt anymore. There was an overflow of sadness in his eyes. Mama and Papa took me to Lander's mother's service. The homegoing was not a big event with a lot of people. There were friends of Lander's and friends of his siblings attending, and that made them all feel better. Lander's supervisor from the post office came, along with some coworkers. Two lady friends of their mother's attended. There was Big Ma and Papa, Jacob and Arlee, Auntie and Joseph, Mama, and me. I was happy that so many in my family supported Lander. He had only been around a few months, and they cared for him already and wanted to be there for him. It was a very intimate and touching graveside service.

Lander asked if we would stand next to him when we first arrived. One of Maria's friends sang their mother's favorite church song, and as soon as she began, Lander grabbed my hand and held it. Lander's uncle from Ohio, who is a preacher, Uncle Lewis, gave a eulogy and said the opening and closing prayers.

Lander's father was there, standing next to his brother, who he had come from Ohio with, and we all could tell he was terribly upset. He held his head down, weeping quietly for most of the time that the service took place. Wilford, surprisingly, had an incredibly angry look on his face, with his eyes constantly on his father. Ruby was talking to him as though she was trying to calm him down about something. I did not see Lander shed any tears that day, but the look on his face was as though his world had ended. Great sorrow was written all over his face.

A few days ago, Papa and Big Ma had told Lander that the after-gathering could be at the family house. Lander was going to pay for a small hall for a couple of hours of fellowship. Papa and Big Ma would not hear of it and told Lander that his family and friends were welcome to all come to the family house for the repast.

When we returned to the family house, Aunt Candy was there with Ruthie and Baby Girl, and they had finished all the cooking and preparation for the grieving family and friends. It was good to see Lander smiling a little and mingling with those who honored his mother. Lander's father and uncle did not join us; they said they needed to get back to Ohio. While our guests were eating and socializing, Lander and I took a stroll on the land. We did not talk very much; he just needed a break away for a few minutes, it seemed.

"I will never forget the love and care that you and your family have shown me, Colleen," Lander said as we sat by the waterfall. "I am so grateful that God sent you into my life. I did not expect Mother to die this soon. They said she had more time. I had planned on her meeting you. She already loved you by the things I told her about you. I thought I had more time, but I didn't." Lander held his head down when he said these things.

I didn't know what to say. I just put his hands in my hands. I did not know what else to do. Lander and I had never kissed, other than a fun peck on the cheek when we said hello and goodbye. At that moment, though, when I had his hands in mine, and I looked deeply into that ocean of sorrow in his eyes, I wanted to kiss him, not on the cheek but on his lips. I think he wanted to kiss me too, but neither one of us made the move.

I know this is a good man, I thought. *He has been so kind to me and everyone that I am close to. In his moments of despair, I feel so helpless.* Before I knew it, I'd put one arm around his waist, lay my head on his chest, broke down, and started crying. I could not hold it anymore. Seeing him hurt like that broke my heart. "You are going to get through this. I promise you will. I am going to make sure. You, Wilford, and Maria are going to be all right! Okay?" I said to Lander, crying and holding him tightly.

Lander had started crying too. He didn't say anything; he just cried. I kept laying my head on his chest, and suddenly, I started singing. I started singing my and Mama's song. It just rose within me. "Safe within. Safe within. Feels so good safe within. I'm in Your palm, in Your palm. I'm engraved within Your palm." I sang the song over and over again, until Lander and I stopped crying, and he hummed along with me. We both ended up humming the song for quite some time. It became so peaceful where we were. Not just the location by the waterfall, but it seemed as if we were in our own private bubble, our own secluded island of love and comfort. Our own world, and in this world, nothing or no one could hurt us.

I held on to him, and he held on to me, and there was nothing—there is nothing—that could break this bond of love and commitment. As we looked in each other's eyes, we knew something had happened to us, something that we dare not speak; it was much too soon.

We walked back to the house, not saying anything, just holding hands tightly. Just as we were getting close, with each step we took, Lander started whispering, "Colleen, I love you. I've loved you from the moment I saw you. I loved you. I love you."

Wobbly Planks

Mama, Auntie, Papa, and Big Ma are sitting at the kitchen table, looking very concerned as I walk in from work. I know immediately that something is wrong.

"Hi, family." I try to say cheerfully, hoping to bring their spirits up with my salutation.

Big Ma and Mama just nod their heads, while Papa says in a worried tone, "Hello, Peaches. How was your day?"

"It was good. Thanks for asking. What's happening here?" I set my belongings down and pull up a chair next to Mama.

"We have problem," Big Ma says, looking at Mama. Tears start to stream down Mama's face.

I grab my mama's hand to hold it and ask, "What's wrong, Mama? Is Daddy all right?"

"It's not your daddy, Peaches. It's Ruthie. Your sister is in a world of trouble," Mama says as she cries harder.

Mama, Big Ma, and Papa explain to me that Ruthie and Baby Girl were in the town store while Papa was in one of his meetings. The girls were there to pick items for Big Ma's projects that we're all going to complete this weekend. Ruthie was arrested for assaulting a young man who recently moved to town with his parents. The officer had her in the adult jail, instead of Juvenile Hall, where a fifteen-year-old should be. The fact that she is not with her age group alone is devasting to Mama and Big Ma. Usually, in the juvenile holding center, families can visit right away, but with Ruthie being in an adult jail, we do not know when we will see her.

Papa is friends with a lot of the lawmen, and one of his friends said for us to come there when he arrives to work, early tomorrow morning. We do not know what the young man's injuries are, but Papa said there was blood and a big mess in the store. Papa paid for some of his workers to clean the store and put it back in order. Papa also paid the shop owner for all the damages.

The shop owner told Papa that the young man was rude and out of hand. He also said that he has had problems in the store with this young man several times since he and his family moved to town. The shop owner and his wife have known Ruthie and all of us girls since we were babies and never had any problem with any of us.

The young man is in the hospital. Papa is going to town shortly to find out as much as he can about the situation. Apparently, when they arrested Ruthie and took her to the jail, they also took Baby Girl to the same building, put her in a holding room, and began questioning her like she was an adult. Papa got to the bottom of it after he and his friend Mr. Perkins got to the jail. My Perkins happen to be in town, and walked into the store when Ruthie was in conflict with the rude young man. Papa wanted to know why they didn't take Baby Girl to the community room at the sheriff's office to wait for him to pick her up, like they were supposed to do since she is a minor.

"Where is Baby Girl?" I ask, since she is nowhere in sight.

"She's in bed; she has just shut down. I don't know what they asked her while they had her in that room, and I don't know why Baby Girl is not opening up to us. This is not like her at all," Big Ma says, getting more excitable.

I can see this has really upset Big Ma, so I smile at her and say, "Let's all calm down. Everything will work out. I'm going to talk to Baby Girl. Everything will get smoothed out. Right, Papa?"

Papa looks up at me, perks up, and replies, "That's right, Peaches. God is working it out; yes, indeed. God is busy right now. Yes, yes, yes."

Walking in the room, I can see Baby Girl with the covers over her head—her way of hiding from the world ever since she slept in the baby bed. I call her name; she does not answer. I call her name again; still, no answer. Acting like I'm leaving the room, I say, "Well, I guess you're not up for talking. I'll chat with you later."

"I'm not asleep," Baby Girl's little scared voice said. Baby Girl's eyes are red and swollen from crying, and her hair is all over her head, and not the 2 neat little ponytails she has every morning.

"Well, it sounds like you and Ruthie were on quite an adventure without me today. Is

that true, little one?" I say, trying to cheer up Baby Girl and get a conversation going at the same time.

"It wasn't an adventure. It was a bad, horrible day, Peaches." Baby Girl says.

I sit at the side of her bed and open my arms, and we hug each other so tightly for a few minutes. As I hold my sweetheart sister, I have to fight back the tears because I am so grateful to God that nothing bad happened to her during the altercation between Ruthie and the young man in the store. I am especially thankful for our Creator for protecting Baby Girl and Ruthie in the entire controversy. It could have ended up much worse for them.

When our people have situations like this, it usually does not end up with such hope. Usually, our people experience the tables being turned on them, and there are tragic endings. *Thank you, God, thank you*, I tell my Creator within my heart.

"The angels were working a lot today, keeping you and sister safe from harm, huh?" I say to remind her of some important things.

Baby Girl takes her arms from around me, sits back, and looks at me. I see in her eyes and in her face the moment it clicked, and she remembers for the first time in her little life what our family has taught us throughout the years about how our Creator will protect us and assign our angels to do the work to keep us from harm.

"Yes, they were, Peaches. I was scared, but I didn't get hurt. I do have angels, and Ruthie too!"

It takes a few minutes of tender loving care and a dose of merriment in our hearts before Baby Girl tells me what happened when they were in the store. Ruthie was looking in the fabric section, and Baby Girl was looking at a new bead selection. A young man came over and started talking to Baby Girl, asking if she wanted some candy. Baby Girl knows what to do and say when she is approached by strangers, and she acted accordingly.

She told the young man no thank you. The young man asked her again, and again, she said no thank you, but he persisted. Ruthie came over and told the young man that the Baby Girl was with her and that she didn't care for any candy.

The young man took offense to Ruthie's saying that to him. He pushed Baby Girl out of the way and stood in front of Ruthie. Ruthie told the young man not to touch her sister again. Baby Girl said that the young man said, "Well, good. I'd rather touch you anyway," and he reached out and touched Ruthie's chest.

Ruthie then told Baby Girl to go over by the front door and wait for her.

"I was too scared to move," Baby Girl says, "because the young man might do something to Ruthie, and I didn't want to leave my sister."

Ruthie took Baby Girl by the hand and walked her over to the front of the counter; the shop owner was standing behind it. Ruthie told Baby Girl not to move from that spot. The young man was still talking crazy to Ruthie, so much so that the shop owner told him to leave the store. Ruthie, realizing this could only get worse, told the storekeeper that she would return and that she was going to find her grandfather. At that time, the young man stepped in front of Ruthie, told her to get out of his way, and shoved her, while throwing a bag of tobacco on the counter. Ruthie demanded that the young man apologize to her baby sister, to the shop owner for disrespecting him, and to her, for his touching her. He laughed at Ruthie and, using more profanity, said he wasn't apologizing. Ruthie then hit the young man in the face and knocked him to the ground.

"I was scared," Baby Girl says, "because Ruthie kept hitting him and kicking him. The shop owner and I were screaming for Ruthie to stop, but she wouldn't. I was so frightened that I began to cry because I knew then that Ruthie was in a lot of trouble—not with just the family but with the law too."

Mr. Perkins, Papa's friend, came in and was finally able to get Ruthie off the young man. Mr. Perkins was kind enough stay there until the sheriff came. Ruthie told Baby Girl to stay with Mr. Perkins until Papa arrived. Mr. Perkins was so kind and walked with my sisters while the lawman took them to the jail and booked Ruthie. Mr. Perkins explained to the lawman that he knew the family and would be happy to take Baby Girl over to where Papa was at his meeting, but the officer refused and made Baby Girl stay in the holding room. Mr. Perkins returned with Papa, but Papa but was not allowed to see Ruthie.

Baby Girl breaks down crying when we're through talking. "Ruthie! They took her away. They took my sister away! I want my sister to come home."

I tell Baby Girl, "It will get better. She'll be back. Now, we must do a lot of praying, asking for God to help us, and He will."

Baby Girl has never been this upset before in her life. How I wanted to always protect her from hurtful things. She has lost some of her innocence, and it breaks my heart. To make her calm down again, I tell her, "I need your assistance in helping Mama, Daddy, Big Ma, and Papa. I need you to help me be strong, so as a sister team, we can get things back to normal. Do you think you can do that for me, Baby Girl? It sure would make things easier for me. Can you?"

I want to make sure she knows how much I need her, and I know I really do. This is new to me. *What if they don't set Ruthie free? How is she feeling right now? I know she is scared in there. Oh God, I hope she doesn't get mad at anyone else. I hope they don't take advantage of her age in there.*

Just as my mind starts going deeper into the tunnel of despair, Baby Girl responds with a confident, "Yes, I'm going to help you. I am a big girl now. I'm not a baby anymore."

We wipe our faces, hug each other one more time, and walk out of the room, ready to do what we have to do to help our family. As we walk out, we can hear Mama and Big Ma out on the front porch. Going out there, I can hear Arlee and Aunt Candy too. They had gotten word of what had happened.

"Where is Papa?" I ask, hoping he hasn't left for town. He

has, and Auntie says that Joseph has taken him. They have been gone quite some time. I didn't realize that Baby Girl and I spent so much time in the bedroom. It feels good to be around all these women that I love. We all have had to be strong in this life, but I am just wondering what the future will be like for Ruthie. Of course, we start cooking and talking and come up with a strategy on how to help Ruthie financially. Papa and Big Ma have a lawyer, and they will go see him tomorrow. We all will make sure she has everything she needs if they keep her in jail.

Aunt Candy says she has some tips she will tell her; she's had a few stays in jail. Aunt Candy is the type of woman who loves really hard and will do anything to help you, especially family. One thing you don't want to do is cross Aunt Candy; that is the wrong thing to do. Arlee told me that she and her mama had a get-together at our cousins' in the next county. They had invited the neighbors to socialize with them; it was men and women there. They were all having fun, all in a big kitchen. Now, there is something about the ladies in our family. We are all sticklers for things to be clean. One of the neighbors was not the neatest person in the world, and he decided that he was going to spit in the kitchen sink. That did not go over well; in fact, it caused such upset for Aunt Candy that she got her cousin's shotgun out of their bedroom and ran the neighbor down the road, past his own house. That gives you an idea about Aunt Candy's temperament.

Arlee has enjoyed living with us at the family house with Big Ma and Papa. It certainly is much calmer than at Aunt Candy's. When everyone is full of food, sun tea, and dessert, we have a time of prayer for my Ruthie. Mama and Big Ma really need the encouragement. We pray, we sing, we cry, we tell jokes, and we do all that we need to do to get through each moment. I slip into the kitchen for a moment alone. As I sit at the kitchen table, I feel totally drained. I have experienced every emotion today, at least it feels like it. How can just one event change our perspective of life so quickly? I must be strong. I must stay focused. Why do I feel like I am going to fall apart? What is wrong with me? Where is this overwhelming feeling of hopelessness coming from? Maybe because Papa and Joseph have been gone for so long, and it's getting very late. This feeling of despair is so strange.

All of a sudden, I hear screaming from the porch—laughter and cries. Just as I am getting out of my chair, Papa walks in, followed by Baby Girl. She is smiling so wide, and behind her is Ruthie. *Ruthie!* Ruthie and I move quickly into each other's arms, and I break down completely. *Oh God, my sister!* We stand there, just holding each other like we will never let go, crying, so happy to be together. We will never take this for granted again.

Baby Girl grabs onto Ruthie and me, crying, saying, "Sisters, sisters, my big sisters!" Just when we feel like we could not feel any more warmth and love, Mama joins in, wrapping her arms around her girls. Big Ma, Auntie, and Arlee wrap around us all before we know it. I can hear Aunt Candy in the background, saying loudly, "Thank You, Lord! I love You, Lord! Thank You!"

Here we are, all of us, drawn like magnets, with all our imperfections and insecurities. We are cemented together, despite our differences, the history of our conflicts, disagreements, and our vulnerabilities. We are here, where we were called to be, with each other, conquering battles. Together, we know that even with all our frailties, we are one huge blend of love and commitment to each other. In our sisterhood is a treasure, like the most precious stone there is. Our blend comes from many heritages and many lands and has many unique and beautiful mixtures. Individually, we may know all that our blend contains, but we may not. Our confidence and pride do not stand only in our ancestry but in the royal priesthood.

The royal priesthood was formed and established by our Creator in our spirit. Our color blend may include Native American, black, brown, red, white, and any other color that God has created through the loins of man. This is what is contained in our womanhood. With all of us standing as one, nothing can beat us, because we each have our Creator. Our Creator has blessed us greatly by giving each of us all power and authority over the circumstances of our lives. More importantly, our Creator has us, and He does not allow anything to happen in our lives that is not in His will and purpose for our lives. Our Creator tells us that He has each one of us engraved in the palms of His hands.

There is not anything that can keep us from His purpose for our lives but us. Therefore, we stand here and hold each other as a confirmation of our commitment to love, truth, and fairness, for each other, and for all those who will cross our paths in our lives. This is what our elders have passed on to us from generation to generation.

Ruthie has been through so much, and I am so happy that she has this knowledge to keep her strong. We are delighted that she is home. Big Ma and Mama bathe her and wash her hair. She needs time with those two. They are using their spiritual and holistic techniques to help Ruthie release anything toxic that took place while she was in jail. All the special attention will promote relaxation, as well as prepare her for the hearing before the judge in just several hours.

The house is quiet. Aunt Candy and Arlee have gone home to rest and freshen up; they will return in time to go to the hearing with us. Baby Girl and Auntie are asleep, and Papa is out on the other end of the porch. I know I should be sleepy, but I am not. I will go out on the porch with Papa. As I approach, I hear voices. *Who is Papa talking to?* I step outside by the rocking chairs, look down at the table at the other end of the porch, and there is Lander!

"Lander, how long have you been here?" I ask in surprise, and I glance at Papa.

Lander, as usual, stands up as I approach. Before Lander can answer, Papa says, "This fellow here has been with me since Joseph and I arrived in town, before we went to see Ruthie."

"How are you, Ms. Colleen?" Lander asks, before I can ask more about what is going on.

I've told Lander he doesn't have to call me "Ms. Colleen" anymore. We have gotten much closer since his mother transitioned. We see each other at least three times a week because he picks me up from work and brings me home. Big Ma always insists on his staying for supper, of course. With school and work, I stay very busy; plus, I don't always want to ride with Arlee and Jacob.

Arlee and Jacob are quite the pair; they need to ride sometime without me tagging along. I have expressed my enjoyment in spending time with Lander; I think I love him, but I really do not know. I will just say that I have very strong feelings for him. I want to stay focused on finishing school and doing the best I can to learn as much as I can at my job.

Sometimes, Lander's sister, Maria, comes with him to pick me up from work and spend the evenings with us. She says her spending time with our family is helping her with the loss of her mother.

Now, I respond to Lander, "I am grateful that Ruthie is home—a little anxious about her hearing today, though." I sit across from him at the table.

"Your mama didn't tell you?" Papa says. I look at him, puzzled. "Peaches, Ruthie does not have court today. Lander, here, talked to that young man's parents, and they have had a change of heart about this entire situation. They aren't pressing charges against your sister. Now, Ruthie is going to have to go to court in a month. She will have to do some community work. I had a long talk to the chief sheriff, and he is aware of what kind a people we are, so he worked with us on the legal part pertaining to the fight. After this court hearing, though, Ruthie will be on probation for a year or so. She cannot get in any trouble because it will be out of our hands to keep her from being locked up. I guess they must have her do something because she hurt that boy pretty bad. The rascal going to be in the hospital for a couple of days. Ruthie broke his nose, and he hit his head on the shop floor awfully hard because he has a head injury. He has a cracked rib too, so I don't think he going to be disrespectful like that anymore. Ruthie going to have to calm herself down. She got to calm herself down."

I don't know what to say. I am so relieved and so thankful that things turned out like this. Papa gets up from the table and reaches out to shake Lander's hand.

Lander stands and extends his hand to Papa.

"Son, you been a true warrior in this situation and the answer to our prayers for Ruthie. I want you to know that from now on, whatever come of you and my granddaughter, here, you will always be welcome in my home. If there is anything I can ever do for you, let me know, and you got it. I don't know what you said to the young man's parents, and I don't need to know. But whatever it was, I never seen so much respect for someone like those people had for you. As a matter of fact, those sheriffs up there got a lot of respect for you. Thanks again. Now I am going to get some sleep. Good night to you both, or should I say good morning."

Lander and I say good night to Papa, and then he sits in the chair next to me. I am so shocked at all Papa said to Lander and all that Lander did. I look at Lander and realize my sister would still be in jail if it weren't for him. Speaking very low, I ask, "Lander, what did you say to make them not press charges against Ruthie?"

"You would be surprised how people will change their minds about things if you make them an offer they cannot refuse." Lander offered the young man's parents a very large sum of money, and they accepted it. Lander had them sign a document saying they would not come back and try to get Ruthie in trouble or try to get more money from Lander.

"How did you get a lot of money?" I ask.

"It was legally," he says right away. "I been working a long time, and I save my money." Lander has said that to me few times. Lander says that Wilford asked him if he wanted Wilford and some of his buddies to pay the young man's father and brother a visit, but Lander fussed at him and told him no; he said that Wilford better stop acting that way before he ends up in jail.

Lander is making me fall more and more for him, and I want to show him I appreciate what he did for Ruthie and my family. I know everyone is in bed for the night, and, most likely, all are asleep. I stand up and take Lander by the hand and lead him to the bench where we can both sit down next to each other. I sit there and just look into those beautiful eyes, and then I kiss him on his lips. It was not a very long kiss, but when I pull my lips off his, he pulls me back to him, and he gives me a long kiss. We sit there for the rest of the night, talking in almost a whisper. I lay with my head on his chest. Lander has his arm around me

"I love you, Lander. I love you so."

Lander looks at me with a surprised face. "Does this mean you are my girl?" Lander asks, looking intent.

"Yes, I am your girl, and you are my guy." I smile at him and squeeze his hand.

Lander turns completely to me and says, "Colleen, I promise I will never hurt you, and I will always protect you."

We kiss a few times more and just enjoy our newly confessed love for one another. I feel so special. He makes me feel this way. He is everything a girl would want in a man. We sit on the porch until sunrise. Lander quietly slips away in his car and drives down the road, and I quietly slip into the house and into my bed.

"Thank you, God," I whisper. "Thank you for all the miracles You have given me and my family."

MH (Mental Health) A state of well being mentally and all it encompasses.

MHC (Mental Health Condition) A illness that affects an individual's thinking, feelings, mood, and behavior.

MHC Trigger: Death of Lander's mother. Lander dealing with the fact that his mother's family disowned him.

MHC Trigger: Ruthie's thought pattern of resolving the issue in a violent way. Ruthie's altercation in town that turned physical and resulted in the hospitalization of the instigator.

MHC Trigger: Ruthie's incarceration and the fact that she will not discuss what happened to her with anyone.

Scriptural Support

The name of the Lord is a strong tower, the righteous run to it, and are safe. (Proverbs 18:10 NKJV)

CHAPTER 5

Uncharted Territory

A lot has happened since that awful day when Ruthie went to jail. Ruthie still does not talk about her experience. She keeps all that happened in that jail locked away inside of her, so no one will know. She has been working at the community center every week and helps with various activities for all age groups. She loves going there and is hoping to get a paying job there one day. I cannot say that her bad temper is gone, but there does seem to be an improvement. Mama and Big Ma try to get her to talk about the incident that led her to the community center, but she just will not. Sometimes she has dreams at night that cause her to yell and fight in her sleep. Mama says to leave her alone when that happens and that we should pray.

Ruthie will talk about a certain young man that brings his great-aunt in to the center during the week. His name is Thomas Baylor. He's five years older than Ruthie, and they both seem smitten with each other. Daddy and Mama gave Thomas permission to court Ruthie, and Big Ma and Papa always keep an eye out when he comes to visit. I like Thomas because he makes Ruthie laugh. Thomas taps into the deep, serious, and irritable part of Ruthie and always manages to pull out a hearty laugh from her. Thomas is an official member of our family house get-together crew, and he fits in fine.

Papa and Big Ma, of course, love it; they love to hear the house full of laughter, the sound of forks hitting plates full of food, the smell of good cooking, and the now-several bottles of sun tea at each dinner. Papa and Big Ma love to see the inquisitive minds and skilled hands of their family members at work on all the baskets, jewelry, blankets, and all the other creations that take place at the family house. Nowadays, it could be on the weekends, weekdays, or both. Big Ma and Papa say the Holy Spirit determines which day and the activities that take place at the family house now.

Arlee and I are almost through with school. She is still planning to become a nurse, and I still want my dress shop. Big Ma said she will help me with my shop, which I think is a wonderful idea. I have learned so much at the dress shop where I work, and I love it. Lander says he is going to build me a shop of my own one day, and I believe him. Every day, I look forward to seeing him, hugging him, and, of course, kissing him. We have begun to talk about having a family one day but not soon. Maria also has gotten close to us; Lander likes his sister being around all of us. She is such a pretty lady, but her real beauty is the person on the inside—gentle spirit, kind, and funny too. When Arlee, Maria, and I go somewhere by ourselves, Maria is the softie that we must look out for in certain situations. Maria, Lander says, is just like his mother. She looks and has ways like her mother.

It is tough for Maria most of the time; she struggles with being accepted by others. She is learning from her sisters that she is fearfully and wonderfully made. She is beautifully unique. Maria is getting stronger and is not as shy as she once was. She is gaining confidence now. Maria was not used to socializing. Her mother was ill for a long time, so she was at home, caring for her and not doing what most young ladies do. She went to high school for two years and then dropped out. Maria says she is going to go back to school one day, but she can write, and she enjoys reading a lot. Arlee and I love her hanging around us. She is a wonderful addition to our sisterhood. She is always so thoughtful, helpful, and sweet; she would not hurt a fly. The three of us do a lot of laughing and acting silly. Big Ma tells us to enjoy our youth because someday, the fun times will not come as often. We have had a taste of responsibility already, with school and work. I am sure it will not be too much different than now.

Road of Darkness

Arlee, Maria, and I are sitting near the springs when Arlee tells us she does not want to go back to her job anymore. Both Maria and I are surprised because Arlee was very satisfied with her job.

"What changed your mind?" I ask her.

"You must promise not to tell anyone," Arlee says.

Arlee and I have kept secrets all our lives, so it's no problem to add another one, I think. Maria and I promise we will keep her secret.

Arlee then tells us, "Lately, Dr. St. Cyr is at home much more than normal, and many times, Mrs. St. Cyr is not there."

"Why is that a problem?" Maria asks. "You're there to take care of the house and the children and don't have to work around Dr. St. Cyr."

Arlee, with a worried look on her face, does not hesitate to say, "Sometimes he follows me around the house. Whatever room I am in alone, he comes in and talks to me. He says things that make me feel extremely uncomfortable." Arlee elaborates on that statement, which causes Maria and me great distress. "The last time I was there, he got close up on me, and I thought he was going to overpower me and make me lie down with him. I was so scared."

Shocked by what Arlee has told us, I loudly say, "Well, you have to tell Aunt Candy! He cannot do that to you. We should tell his wife; we must do something!"

"No, no!" Arlee shouts. "If Mama finds out, she will kill him. She might end up in jail for the rest of her life, or she might be killed. We cannot tell Mama or anyone. We can't say anything to any of our folks. It will cause big problems for our family. There is not anything our folks can say or do to help me. We are colored, and no one with lawful authority will help me—no one. I must figure this one out by myself. Look what happened to Ruthie— that boy was out in the open with his foolishness, and Ruthie still went to jail!" By this time, Arlee is crying, and we are crying right along with her.

We all sit there, feeling helpless, and I tell Arlee that we were going to figure it out. I realize that this man has terrorized my Arlee, my sweet sister. I look at Arlee and say, "You cannot go back there. We won't let you go back there. God, our Creator, is with us. He will give us a way of escape—always."

Suddenly, Maria, who has been silent through most of this conversation, looks at me intently and says very boldly and definitely, "We have to tell Lander and Wilford. They will know what to do. They are experts at solving all kind of problems, especially these."

When Maria said "especially these," she gave me a look I'd never seen before. It's a look that says things with her eyes that she cannot say verbally. We look at each other in silence for what seems like two or three minutes.

I then think of how Lander and Wilford helped Ruthie. *Surely, they will be able to help us.* I suggest we pray, and we join hands and do exactly that. We pray that our Creator will show us what to do. He always does, and He will help us this time. No matter what it looks like, we will get through this.

We all decide that some of Big Ma's peach cobbler and ice cream is needed right now. We return home and sit on the porch with our elders. I look at each one of them and think about all that they have been through in their lives. Arlee is right; we cannot be careless and allow her situation to rob our elders of the good days they have left and the happy times they have earned.

After our dessert on the porch, Maria, Arlee, and I experiment with a new hairstyle, which gives us more time to talk in private.

I tell Arlee to trust us. Looking directly into her eyes, I say, "You cannot go back to that house, Arlee. I will talk to Lander, and we will figure everything out. Find a reason not to go to work on Monday—a reason that will keep you out for some days so it won't draw attention. We will figure out everything else."

Arlee seems relieved that someone else is involved in her horrible situation. We have learned from our elders that we cannot take the normal and legal way for justice to help us when we have problems. The fact is that the law looks down on us, does not see us as equals, and does not value us. Their answers to resolving problems in life are not the right answers for us. As people of color, it could cost us many things—our freedom, our lives, or the lives of those who love us.

One big mistake my people often make is that when intimidated or victimized, to protect our loved ones from getting in involved and possibly in trouble, we keep silent. Silence and secrets are the culprits that will destroy the mind, body, and soul, if allowed to take residence within someone who is being victimized. Silence and secrets take many people hostage, and they are never free until they let go of the secrecy.

I am glad Arlee trusted Maria and me and did not allow her life to be held captive by an evil man who preys on young girls. We definitely cannot let Ruthie know of this situation; she would be highly upset and take actions into her own hands, which would jeopardize her freedom and cause even more heartache in the family. There is no telling what Ruthie and her hot-headed self would do.

Later, as I lie in the bed, looking out the window, my heart, mind, and the entirety of my soul cries out to my Creator to help me, to show me what to do to help Arlee. She is pure and innocent and has the right to choose to whom she gives herself for the first time or any time. This is a right that has been denied to many women of color. There are times when most of us women of color do not do the extra things to enhance our beauty. In fact, we do the opposite, especially when we are going to be around others who are not our family. We have been taught by our women elders how to cover our bodies with clothing to avoid the unwanted looks of men. We keep our bodies and hair in a way that does not draw the attention of others.

We have many tricks to conceal our beauty. Yes, much has been stolen from women of color and has caused each woman monumental pain. As Big Ma says, no matter how we are breaking on the inside, we know how to hide it on the outside, and it will not show on our faces. We have been taught possible ways to prevent unwanted looks and advances that work for us sometimes. Many times, our women who do not have family or a support system are at the mercy of those who disrespect and take advantage them. Because many in this land do not value women of color as they value other women, our being victimized is most times turned into something that we did wrong to cause the disrespect. That prevents many women from seeking justice, and many suffer in silence that destroys, and they never share the attacks against them.

Arlee will not be one of these women. I talk to my Creator all night. He tells us to spend time with Him and talk and be real with Him, as we would with our best friend in times of need and help. When I spend time with my Creator, He tells me exactly what to do, when I sit still and listen to Him. When I do this, it puts me in a position for success, to win, despite the magnitude of the circumstances.

I had only a few hours of sleep because I am so anxious to see Lander and to tell him what is going on. He will be here early this afternoon. Since it is Saturday, I will sleep longer, rest my mind, and rest my body.

When Lander arrives, we immediately walk down by the spring and sit down. I explain what Arlee told Maria and me. Lander is visibly upset and concerned about the situation. He feels very protective of Arlee and asks many questions. I had the answers to some questions; some, I did not. Lander asks me to get certain information from Arlee. He needs to know which hospital Dr. St. Cyr works at because he does not work at our hospital in town. He is employed in another county. Lander also needs to know when he works and any other information about where Dr. St. Cyr frequents.

When we get up from the ground, Lander takes me in his arms, kisses me, and then gives me the tightest hug he has given me ever. "I will be back," he says, "and I promise you this will be resolved, all right? Have Arlee ready with that information. Okay, Peaches? I will return in a few hours."

He walks at a fast pace in front of me toward the house.

I try to walk fast enough to catch up with him. "Lander," I call out, "wait a minute. What are you going to do? Lander?"

Lander stops and turns around. "Do you trust me, Peaches? Do you know that I will do anything to keep your family out of harm's way? Do you know I would never do anything to jeopardize this wonderful relationship we have, something that I have waited for all my life? Do you, Peaches? Do you trust me?"

I can see that Lander is intent on my answering his questions. With confidence, I honestly say, "Yes, I trust you, Lander. Yes, I do trust you."

"Then you must know that there will be some things that I cannot discuss with you, things that are not necessary for you to know. That is the way things must be. All right, dear?"

I look into Lander's eyes, and I know he was speaking about the uncharted territory in his life, things that he wants to protect me from. "Yes, yes. I understand what you are saying, and I am with you on this." I say this confidently as I pull back and point for him to go ahead, where he was going before I interrupted. Lander gives me a peck on the cheek and takes off faster than he had been walking before I stopped him.

I watch as he leaves, all the way to the gate, and when he turns left on the road, I can't do anything but plop on the grass, right where I am. I thank God that He has answered my prayer through Lander. I know it will all work out; it has to work out. I walk back to the family house to talk to Arlee and get the information that Lander needs.

Later, in the early evening, Lander returns, and Maria,

Wilford, and Joseph are with him. They all huddle at the table at the end of the porch. Lander asks Arlee and me to take a walk with him down to the springs. When we get there, Lander thanks Arlee for trusting him and for relaying the information he asked for. Lander apologizes for Dr. St. Cyr's horrible behavior and promises Arlee that things will get better for her.

Arlee doesn't say much, other than to give Lander all the information. Toward the end of the conversation, when Lander says he's sorry that this has happened to her, Arlee cries, but he promises things will get better. Maria walks down to the springs and suggests that Arlee eat something. Arlee has not eaten all day. Big Ma noticed and wondered what was wrong with her and why she has no appetite. Big Ma notices all the happenings with us but rarely says anything about it. We find out later that she was on to us.

Maria and Arlee walk back to the house, while Lander and I sit on the grass, looking at the springs.

"Peaches, I won't be here to spend the day and have Sunday dinner tomorrow. Some unexpected things have come up that need my attention." Lander said these things without looking at me, just keeping his eyes fixed on the springs.

I realize that this is the first of what I believe is going to be "uncharted territory" in our relationship. I too look straight ahead at the springs as I softly whisper, "I understand. I will miss you tomorrow. Just please always be safe, and look to God for any help you need."

Lander gets up and walks to the house. I sit there, still looking at the springs, knowing something big is about to happen. I know everything will get resolved, and I also know that God has sent a mighty soldier into our family. Now it is time for me to soldier up because I am going to marry this man; together, we can care for and protect our family.

Big Ma has always told us that, as strong women, we should have a relationship with God and a skill to make a living. We should do the things that make us happy, and if it is God's will, we will have husbands. Big Ma teaches us not to totally depend on our husbands but to consider them a bonus, love them, work together, and build happy lives with them. That is what I want. I love Lander. He is such a good man, and I will not let him slip out of my arms—ever.

The men are huddled on and off the lawn all evening, and at some point, Papa and Daddy join them. They are all at the fishing spot, with chairs and drinks. Their conversation seems intense and sometimes boisterous. The ladies on the porch don't know what is going on, but Arlee, Maria and I know.

The men call it an early night, which is unusual. Papa sits on the porch just a little while but retires to his room early as well. It was a good Saturday night; we were busy with all our activities, but my conversation with Lander was on the top of my mind all evening. I wondered what would take place.

Arlee, Maria, and I ease our way to our bedroom for time by ourselves, leaving Big Ma, Auntie, Baby Girl, Ruthie, and Aunt Candy on the porch. We try to assure Arlee that everything will be all right, but it's too hard for her to understand. Arlee eventually goes to sleep, which is a relief for Maria and me.

Sunday goes by fast. We help Big Ma with canning and sewing after our Sunday home church service. Big Ma has started to slow down a little. The doctor says she has heart problems but nothing serious.

Arlee tells Big Ma she feels tired and will be home for a few days this week. Big Ma doesn't ask why; she is simply happy to hear that. I am aware that Big Mas knows something is going on, but she respects Arlee's privacy and does not inquire.

Everyone goes on with their week, which is uneventful. By Wednesday, I request time off to spend the rest of the day after school with Arlee.

Later, Mama and Auntie come in with surprising news. "Arlee! We are so glad that you did not go to work today!" says Auntie.

Arlee looks up, surprised. "Why?"

"There was an explosion and a fire today at the St. Cyr's

mansion!" Mama says excitedly. "Their neighbors said that they recently had switched over to natural gas heating, and something went wrong. They just had it put in last month, didn't they, Arlee?"

Arlee says she remembers the home being busy last month, with workers in and out of the house. "The gas heater, which appeared to be more like a furnace, took up a lot of space—so much so that Mrs. St. Cyr had to take some pieces of furniture out of the room so it would not be crowded." Arlee sighs and asks with great concern, "Was anyone hurt?"

"No one was home," Mama says in a reassuring voice. "The house burned to the ground. There is nothing left but ashes. I don't think many people will want to have natural gas installed in their homes now. It's too risky!"

I am stunned. In my mind, I wonder, *Was it the natural gas, or was it the anger and exasperation of a desperate people, seeking their own justice?*

"Well, Arlee, honey, look like you are going to have to find other work. There is nothing to go back to. Do you think they will buy another home in the area?" Big Ma asks.

"The neighbor isn't sure but said that Mrs. St. Cyr didn't want to move here in the first place and wants to go back and live near her parents and other family. That might be idle gossip, but they have a lot to think about. To start all over, with nothing, won't be easy, even if they do have money. Emotionally, that must be awful," Mama says, shaking her head.

I sit at the kitchen table because my legs suddenly feel weak. *Is this really happening?*

Arlee can't control herself and bursts into tears, crying, "Oh my goodness, oh my goodness!"

Big Ma moves to Arlee quickly and holds her, saying, "Arlee don't you worry about anything. You will get another job. And as far as your completing school and the celebrations, Papa and I have already talked about helping your mother with everything you need. You do not have to worry about your nursing school either. All that will be taken care of. You hear, baby?"

Arlee nods her head between sobs, but I know her tears are possibly because of shock. Arlee has been thrown into a reality that has changed her already and affected her life greatly. To know that the storm she has been in is over should be a relief, yet there is the confusion of not knowing what really happened. Was it by some twist of fate that the house burned down because of the installation of the gas heater? Was this the result of Arlee's safety and honor being defended? One thing is certain: we won't know anything until we talk to Lander, and he has not been around this week, which is unusual.

Arlee and I sit on the porch, watching the sunset. Without saying a word, Arlee and I know our lives have changed. We want to go back to the way it was before Ruthie's fight and before this threat that Arlee had to live through. I think of that protective curtain across the world that Big Ma and Papa have been pulling back slowly for years. I believe that curtain is almost completely open now. There could not be too much more to learn about life. I know that this is only the beginning. I know we will make it—why wouldn't we? We have our family; we are together through good and bad times. We, as a family, have some freedoms, but most of all, we have our Creator, who is with us every moment. Yes! Our future is awesome! I see it with my eyes of faith.

The months seem to fly by. Arlee has withdrawn from the outside world. If she isn't with Jacob, she is at Aunt Candy's, or she is right here at the family house with Papa and Big Ma. Arlee says she's going to wait a while to get another job, so Big Ma and Papa pay her an allowance for all she does around the family house to help them. Arlee does not like leaving home anymore. She feels like people are watching and talking about her all the time. Aunt Candy tells Arlee that if she doesn't look at people, she won't see them looking at her.

Arlee says she doesn't want to go to nursing school anymore, for some unknown reason. She feels she would not make a good nurse. Ruthie says that Arlee doesn't believe in herself anymore, and I say that we are going to change that!

**MH (Mental Health) A state of well being
mentally, and all it encompasses.**

**MHC (Mental Health Condition) A illness
that affects an individual's thinking,
feelings, mood, and behavior.**

MHC Trigger: Maria dealing with her ethnicity and the rejection of her mother's family. Stepping out on her own and making new a life for herself, outside of the caregiver role she was accustomed to having with her mother.

MHC Trigger: Arlee trying to cope with the fact that her employer feels he can take advantage of her. Arlee's fear of possibly being assaulted.

MHC Trigger: Colleen's stress and anxiety in finding a way to help Arlee.

MHC Trigger: Arlee having mixed emotions—upset, relieved, and feeling guilty—regarding the fire her employer's home.

MHC Trigger: Arlee withdrawn, introverted, feeling self-conscious about others looking at her or talking about her.

Scriptural Support

> Trust in the Lord with all your heart, and do not lean on your own understanding. In all your ways acknowledge Him, and He will direct your paths. (Proverbs 3:5–6 NKJV)

> Casting all your cares on Him, for He cares for you. (1 Peter 5:7 NKJV)

CHAPTER 6

Destiny

L
ander has asked Mama, Daddy, Big Ma and Papa if he could have my hand in marriage. He told them that he wanted to spend the rest of his life with me and that he would stand by my side all my life. Arlee, Ruthie, Baby Girl and I were all listening in the hallway, outside the living room; it was exciting.

Of course, all my elders approved of the marriage. Lander has become one of the family already. Lander and Papa have become remarkably close; they do a lot at the house, as well as go to meetings in town.

When Lander asked me to marry him, he had help from the ladies and set up a beautiful dinner by the springs. Big Ma had her cleaned, pressed, white linen tablecloth on the table, with two large candelabras and two vases full of Big Ma's flowers from her garden. It was a wonderful evening. Lander did so much to make each moment special. Lander told me that he wanted us to discuss our future life.

Lander said that he had found property where he would like to build a home for us. "I would like for you to see the land. I think you will like it. I want us to be married, live at the house, have children, and spend the rest of our lives there."

I did not hesitate to tell Lander yes, that I was ready. We were both excited about our future. Lander told me that his idea for a house was different from a traditional family house. He wants to build what they called a triplex. A triplex is one building with three apartments in it. Each apartment will have all the things a large family will need—living room, kitchen, dining room, indoor bathroom with bathing accommodations, two bedrooms, and a porch.

Lander thinks that's an effective way to help our family stay close as we grow. Lander also feels that it's important that Mama and Daddy be as near to us as possible as they get older, which makes good sense. We will know later who will take the third apartment. Lander says that it's all about timing.

"It all sounds wonderful, Lander. You have thought of everything," I said as I reached for his hand.

"I want you to be part of the decision-making process on how the apartments will look," he said.

It will be wonderful. There is much to do. Lander wants to build the house so that when we marry, we will live there at once. We will live a happy life there and have a lot of children. I am praying that Arlee will come out of this slump she is in. I want everyone to be as happy as I am. We must leave behind the negative circumstances that have happened and move forward to a better life. If I must be the one to encourage my loved ones to see the good in life, so be it.

Lander and I have decided to marry after I finish school, so we have plenty of time to plan and prepare. Big Ma and Papa were thrilled when Lander and I asked if we could get married at the family house. Lander and I love this place. It is so fitting that we marry on the grounds where we really got to know each other and fell in love. There is enough room for the ceremony, the tables, and a place for dancing.

Big Ma, Mama, and Auntie started on my wedding dress as soon as I decided what I wanted. I want my dress to be a fitted gown with long, sweeping lines—that is the latest style, and it is very elegant. I need something that's slimming, since I am not one who will hold back on any of the good meals we have at the family house. I saw exactly what I wanted in the *Vogue* pattern book at work.

The dress will have a high neckline, with long sleeves made from French lace, with a silk slip. The entire dress will be beaded with white pearls, and I will wear a half-sleeve bridal breast plate that is traditionally worn by both African and Creek women, embroidered and beaded with all the bright and beautiful African and Muscogee colors. I will wear my hair back in a bun, with a hair ornament that Ruthie, Arlee, and Baby Girl are making for me. The hair ornament is a thin gold vine that goes around my head. It is slightly beaded with small gold beads and accented with small golden feathers, to honor Papa's mother, Great-Grandmother Golden Feather. I feel such a connection with her.

Also, for that day, Papa is making a white moccasin-type slipper for me that will be beaded to match my breastplate. The breastplate and footwear, Big Ma has taught us, is especially important for a bride to wear. The breastplate represents the protection our Creator gives me to protect my heart throughout my life, so that it can be strong and prevent it from breaking into pieces throughout my adult life as a wife and a mother and in every role I have. The footwear is a symbol of how my Creator and His Word will be a lamp to my feet and a light to my path. Both the breastplate and the slippers will have turquoise as the dominant stone, as well as the other African and Creek stones. I don't mind hearing suggestions from my family; this is not just my wedding but a special time for all the family to come together and celebrate who we are and how we are all connected.

My elders always tell me to treasure each moment with the ones I love, with my friends and family, because I may never get that chance again. To be able to laugh, eat together, and show love and support for one another is a precious gift from our Creator. Mama says if we show love and kindness all the time to those we care for, then we will have no regrets, no matter what happens suddenly. So many of our ancestors never knew that the time they had together was their last time together. Those who came before me would never see or hear from their loved ones, ever again. To not know what happened to family or friends, to wonder if your loved one is living or dead, is a sad empty experience that I pray that we, as family and friends, will never have to go through.

I have been wanting to get my nose pierced, off and on for years, so Mama and Daddy surprised me with two different genuine stones for my nose—a ruby for special occasions and a turquoise for everyday wear. Mama and Daddy are going to take me to get my nose pierced by one of Big Ma's Bible-study friends. Big Ma could do it, but she has her hands full with making my dress and getting the house and land ready for the wedding.

There would not be preparations for the wedding, if it were not for my family. Between finishing school, working, and preparing for the new property, my hands also are quite full. I am not complaining, though. My Creator says He will do exceedingly more than what I can ask or think, and that is certainly what He is doing in my life.

It did not take long for Lander, Papa, and the workers to get started on the apartments. The land where they're building is so beautiful. Green grass in the front; grass and trees in the back. There is a medium-sized stream flowing through the back of the property. Plenty of room in the backyard for a garden and, of course, a place for our future children to play.

Daddy and Mama are packing up their house slowly. Auntie says she will stay with Big Ma and Papa after Mama and Daddy move. Of course, Arlee will be there with Big Ma and Papa too. My job is wonderful, and nothing will have to change after getting married and moved. My boss has taught me so many things. Between Big Ma and my boss, I have learned enough to create my own designs now.

Papa likes the idea of me selling my own creations. He says that the only way for people of color to get ahead financially is to have their own businesses. We must be wise and careful about not having too much exposure. It could cause resentment and multiple problems. It would not please some people to know that we are prospering. Papa and Lander are already talking about building me a dress shop on the land. Papa said that they will build a fence around the house where we'll live. The dress shop would be farther down the road but not too close to the house.

Everyone is getting excited about all that is happening. Big Ma and I have been teaching Arlee some things about sewing and creating blankets, bedspreads, and curtains as well. Big Ma says that since the ladies will be in the shop, buying clothes for their families, we might as well have things for the house too.

Ruthie is becoming more relaxed. She doesn't act as mean as she used to be. I know it has a lot to do with Thomas and his patient self. She has been consistent in going to school so we are hoping she will finish and graduate, like Arlee and I are going to do. Education is very important; our elders have taught us that. When you learn to do things with your mind, no one can ever take that away from you. Being able to read, write, and have math skills, along with good home training, can take us places that our people have never been before. We all laugh because we know that whenever we talk about our future, Papa always has this little saying: "Work today to change your and your children's tomorrows." We have heard that from Papa throughout all our years of growing up. Now, I get to put it into action Papa's sayings, and nothing will stop me. Our people have worked so hard and made so many sacrifices for the generations that will come after them.

With all the planning, completing school, and making sure everyone is in a good place and happy, the time flies by.

Commitment Day of Joy

The wedding was more than what I dreamed of. Papa and Big Ma went all the way to make it wonderful for Lander and me. All our family was there. There were so many—my boss and her family, Lander's family and work friends. It was wonderful. My daddy walked me down the aisle, but Papa was the one who really walked me down the aisle, the aisle of my life leading up to that moment. Papa, Mama, Big Ma, and Auntie all did.

My daddy—I love him, and I want only the best for him. He is a good man. I do not minimize anything he has done for me in my life. If it were not for him, I would not be here, for he gave me life, and I will honor him all my life. I will be perfectly clear, though, that as much as I love him, because of his actions when I was a child, I grew up being afraid of him. That fear overpowered the opportunity for us to have a close relationship for a long time. I am happy that the empty part in my heart that was left unfulfilled for so long is being filled now with Daddy and me, working toward a father/daughter bond now. I accept my relationship with my daddy as it is, and I leave that part of our relationship that we missed out on, on the unanswered, unfulfilled jar shelf, in the pantry of my life, as Big Ma has taught me.

He walked me down the aisle because it would hurt him deeply if he did not. I do not judge my daddy because I have not walked in his shoes or gone through the things he has gone through. Daddy is my daddy. I love him, and I never want anything to hurt him. I want all my family to be happy and proud of me.

To honor my Papa, after my first dance with Lander, Papa and I danced two dances. The first one was a slow dance, and during that dance, Papa shared how proud he was of me and that I am one of the biggest joys of his life. We talked about all the things he and I overcame together while I was growing up. I thanked Papa for all he has done for me and what he continues to do for me. Papa and I have a special relationship. I was his first grandchild, and he was the first man I loved. Papa said that when my daughter has her wedding, he and I will dance like this again and share about even more things that we have experienced in life.

Our second dance was our silly dance. Neither one of us can fast-dance, but we made up our own dance moves, like we always did while I was growing up. We made Big Ma join us in our fast dance, and she added a real spark to our dance. At one point, Papa took turns twirling each us around until the dance was over. At the end of the dance, Papa, as a gentleman, bowed down to Big Ma and me to show it was an honor for him to dance with us. That is a gesture from England that Grandfather Clarence taught Papa when he danced with his mother, Golden Feather.

Dancing with my grandparents is one of the highlights of my wedding day, and I will never forget it. I treasure every moment I spend with Papa and Big Ma, and I am looking forward to the three of us experiencing wonderful moments together with my children.

The treasure of family is marked by each moment together, whether it is a special occasion or not. Each challenge, each success, and each bond that we make shows what we value. Sharing life experiences and relying on family has been a foundation that has made me who I am. I have been taught that if there ever comes a time when we cannot be together—any of us—that we also know each other by the spirit, and by the spirit, we will always be united. By the spirit, we will always be together in our hearts, our minds, and in our memories.

I am proud of who I am—me, with all my blended blood. God made me special, and I will not let God down or let my family down. My happiness will be their happiness; my achievements and my prosperity will be theirs. This is what Papa and Big Ma have done and their parents before them.

All that I know of my ancestors continued to be in my thoughts on the day Lander and I made our commitment to one another. On our wedding day, and every day since then, I feel like I am standing on the shoulders of all who have come before me. My blessed life is the result of all my ancestors' hard work—from the floor of that slave ship that my grandfathers lay on for months, coming across the ocean, to the sorrow of my great-grandmother Golden Feather. Great-grandmother Golden Feather shed many tears when her uncle Chief Brown Horse and the clan were sent away from their land. Sent to a land unknown to them, a land that most of them never even reached because the journey was so perilous. They lost so much, yet they kept going and did not give up, even though, with pride and dignity, they walked into their deaths.

For all the sadness, demanding work, fortitude, and unfulfilled dreams, I dedicated my wedding day and the rest of my life to all who have suffered the sting of injustice. Any success I will ever have will be because of my Creator and my people who have come before me. Despite the society we live in, I will never have any shame for who I am and where I come from. Whatever negative things that are said to me or done to me, I will take that as a badge of honor. I will teach my children and my children's children—from generation to generation until the end of time—that we are a beautiful, unique tapestry that makes great contributions to this life and this world.

I do not know what lies ahead of me since my wedding day, but whatever it is, my Creator, Lander, and my colored, blended, Negro, Muscogee (Creek) folks love me and are with me. These gifts are the greatest treasures of my life.

I think often about all of the exciting moments on my wedding day, that makes me feel so happy. Right before the ceremony, Lander, who is a very confident, masculine man, on that day, I heard that he was extremely nervous and excited.

While I was putting on my wedding attire, Big Ma said "That poor Lander is shaking like a leaf on a tree. Wilbur is just as bad as his brother, and he is not any help at all in calming Lander". Big Ma said as she chuckled. Memories of Aunt Candy made me laugh, with her comments on all the handsome men who were arriving. She belted out loudly to us girls, "Oh, y'all better be glad I am not thirty years younger. I would be embarrassing all of you today—for sure I would! Whew, I am feeling a little faint right now!" Aunt Candy was quite pumped up saying this when she came into the dressing room.

I looked at Ruthie, and we started laughing because Arlee

had that look that she always has on her face when her Mama is about to embarrass her. Aunt Candy is wonderful to be around because she is extra happy and likes getting the atmosphere in a joyful mode of fun and laughter. Aunt Candy gets things going in a happy direction with her unique and spontaneous actions. Arlee's facial expressions and body language showed she was not pleased with her mother.

Aunt Candy looked at Arlee and said, "Now, Arlee, don't you start looking at me like that. You leave me alone today; you hear me? This is Peaches's wedding day, and I'm about to have me some fun, like I haven't had in a long time! Who has some sweet perfume for me to put on? That's all I have left to do—to smell sweet; sweet as a flower."

Ruthie handed Aunt Candy a bottle of perfume off the dresser.

"Oh yes, thank you, baby," Aunt Candy said, "because the bees are coming for the honey today."

"Mama, please!" Arlee said, rolling her eyes at her mother.

"Arlee, you better stop being so doggone rigid, and enjoy life. You need to take some lessons from your mama! Let me get out of here before you make me mad. I got to go and get me a sip of that fancy wine y'all got out there. I also need to make sure all your guests are comfortable. You know what I mean, Peaches?" Aunt Candy said, looking at me, smiling, and winking. "Peaches, girl, it's your day, baby. Don't let any of those high-society folks that's sitting out there get on your nerves. But if they do, let me know, and I'll take care of them. I'm going to be keeping an eye on you all day anyway, for your mama, and if you need anything, just signal for me, OK? You know I will take care of anything, won't I, baby?"

Before I could answer her, Aunt Candy walked out the door, wearing her big turquoise hat with the big flower on it, swishing her hips back and forth, which she doesn't ever do unless she feels rather good about herself.

As I continue to think back on the wedding day, I remember that I had been getting nervous, but after Aunt Candy came in, all I could do was smile and enjoy the moments that were taking place and would never come again. What would a special occasion be like without Aunt Candy and her ways? I love her fun spirit that always has lightened the mood, ever since I can remember.

Ruthie was my marriage sponsor, and Wilford was Lander's marriage sponsor. Ruthie, Arlee, Maria, and Baby Girl's dresses are made exactly like my dress, only theirs were made from turquoise French lace, with pearl and rhinestone beading all over the dresses, so that each dress shimmers and shines. They didn't have a beaded breast plate, as my dress did, but they had a chiffon, turquoise, short-sleeve jacket to wear on top. I choose turquoise dresses for all the ladies because it is Mama's and Big Ma's favorite color. They were wearing their hair in different styles, but all had golden feather hair combs that have pearls and rhinestone beading on them.

Mama, Big Ma, and Auntie went with similar colors as well— Mama with an organza mother-of-the-bride dress and Big Ma in a gorgeous turquoise, A-line, formal dress with a matching long coat. All three wore their hair down for a change. And they all looked beautiful. Papa wore a double-breasted cream suit and a navy dress shirt, with a navy-and-white tie. Papa had his hair back in a large braid down past his shoulder . Everyone looked more beautiful than I could have ever imagined.

Outside was the perfect setting for Lander and me to marry. Papa and his workers had everything looking so amazing. Lander and I exchanged our vows while facing the springs, where we have spent our most intimate times together. The seating for guests during the marriage ceremony and the reception was set up in such a way that they were able to see and hear the waterfall the entire event . Water is very important to us, so that was a big part of the wedding day. Big Ma had sage and lavender packets burning near each guest table. Papa's friends were taking turns playing the flute when the band Lander hired took breaks.

Lander looked so fine and handsome that day that I could hardly believe that this man was going to be my husband. Lander wore a sharp, custom-made, navy double-breasted suit, a white dress shirt with gold cufflinks, and blue-and-white silk tie. His smile was the highlight of my day. Out of all the things that stood out the most that day, was Lander's smile. I never saw him smile like that before. All I saw was Lander's smile when Daddy walked me down the aisle. When I reached Lander, standing there, we were both crying a little.

I love and trust him so much, and I know he will never let me down in our life together. The beautiful part about our love is that we are true to who we are as individuals. We each have our own thoughts, dreams, and passions, and we each do not make our own, as individuals, more important than the other's. I am not naïve to think that we will not have problems in life, but I do believe that whatever lies ahead, we will get through it together, like how Daddy and Mama, Big Ma and Papa, Grandfather Clarence and Grandmother Golden Feather did.

Before we made our vows to each other, we had the washing-of-our-hands ceremony. This is a Creek custom at weddings, where it is a symbol of purification and cleansing. We wash our hands in a bowl together to wash away anything evil and to wash away any memories of previous lovers. Lander's Uncle Luke from Ohio came to town to officiate our wedding ceremony. Lander's father, also came with Uncle Luke. Uncle Luke read from the Holy Bible in Corinthians what love was and admonished us to stay together through thick and thin. He was exceedingly kind and seemed sincere in saying that marriage is a great union but—and he put emphasis on this fact—it takes a lot of work for the marriage to last.

Lander and I had talked about this before we even thought of getting married. He spoke on his parents' marriage, and I spoke on Mama and Daddy's marriage. While we both love our parents, we agreed there are some things in our parents' marriages that we do not want to duplicate. Lander and I exchanged our vows, and it was very touching. I managed to get through it the rest of the vows without crying, and I repeated the vows correctly.

The last part of our ceremony, before the benediction prayer, was the drinking from the wedding vase. This vase is also a custom from both Papa's and Big Ma's family. The vase stands for two people becoming one, and we were helped by Big Ma and Papa. As they walked up to us, I began to cry the hardest in the entire ceremony, just out of all the love I have in my heart for them. They have made such an enormous impact on my life, and I am so happy and grateful that they were right there with me at that moment. I will be forever grateful for all the love they poured into my life and now into Lander's life. I want so much to be the type of grandparent they have been to me; that is one of my greatest goals in life.

After my grandparents helped us with the drinking from the vase, Uncle Luke pronounced us man and wife. At this point, Ruthie and Wilford brought the beautiful broom that Baby Girl, Ruthie, and I decorated and placed it in front of us. Ruthie held one end of the broom, and Wilford held the other end. Joined by our hands, Lander and I had to jump over the broom into married life, which is a tradition from both Lander's and my African family. I was so shaky from all the emotions flowing that I hoped I would not embarrass Lander by falling over the broom instead of jumping over it! It's not that easy to jump a broom while holding your new spouse's hand at the same time. *Oh well, here we go. One, two, three …*

We were now Mr. and Mrs. Lander Banks!

CHAPTER 7

Test of Strength

I love sitting on my porch as the sun is rising. There's something about it that gives me a sense of expectancy. I love it because it gives me hope, even in the little things. It gives me another chance to possibly change the things that happened in my yesterdays. Whether negative or positive situations, I have the option to do something different to something or to some situation. Having those options can be as minor as changing the color of something or rearranging furniture to open a room up. Having options for change can be as serious as how I treat all the people in my life by what I say and how I say it. What do my body movements and facial expressions say to the people in my life?

In the two years that Lander and I have been married, I have found out all these things have a greater significance and have a greater importance in my life. Having my morning devotional time with my Creator is one way I can stay on track with things in life. When I was not doing it, I was just floating through each day, and many times, I really messed things up without even realizing it.

Lander and I get along well. He is a very confident person who knows what he wants for himself and his loved ones, and he moves forward with a defined, strategized plan—it gets done, and that's it. I have my plans, but I do not do all that. I know what

I must do, and I just do it. The fact that we have two different outlooks on how to deal with things and how to get things done was, at first, a little annoying to me. The annoyance did not come from our having the two different styles but from Lander always giving his opinion on how he thinks I should do some things and telling me how he would do it if it was his choice. Other than dealing with that issue and the process of getting it resolved, we have gotten along well, and we are enjoying our life.

Mama and Daddy moved into the apartment on the end. It has been nice having my parents so close to me, especially since Lander and I had our first child a year ago, a girl whom we named Esther Maureen. We named her after Esther in the Bible and Big Ma, whose name is Maureen. She is a happy baby. Lander spoils her when he comes home. Mama does not work anymore because she has health issues. Lander said we shouldn't charge my parents rent. My parents are getting older, and we can see the toll of working for years starting to show.

Daddy's work with the railroad is still the same, other than that he and the workers have been complaining to the company about the conditions on the tracks. The United States government, which controls the railroads, had a Labor Board with authority to hear any disputes the railroad workers had. Railroad services increased when the diesel engines replaced the steam engines. The diesel-engine trains were much easier to maintain than the steam engines they replaced. In addition to being easier to support, the speed of the train increased greatly.

Daddy and Mama had a few discussions with Lander and me about the problems that Daddy and his coworkers had at work. Daddy's job at the railroad was to repair the tracks the trains run on. For many years, there were complaints that colored workers were getting injured, and some were killed because there was not proper lighting at night on the tracks. Daddy says he's going to retire in five years; he will have a good retirement. He and Mama are planning on traveling to see the entire country.

It is so nice to have little Esther be so close to her grandparents.

Mama was at my house during the day with Esther while Daddy slept during the day. When I went to work, I had peace because Esther was in the comfort of her home, with her grandma giving her the best of care.

I did not have a regular schedule anymore at the shop. A retail clerk was hired to assist customers in the shop, while I design and make the items for the customers. I am now responsible for all the orders that come in and the accounting. Arlee also works at the dress shop part-time because she finally decided to attend nursing school. It took Arlee quite some time to get her confidence back after the intimidation and fear she experienced with Dr. St. Cyr.

The fact that the St. Cyr home burned to the ground also changed Arlee, and she has never talked to me about it. Arlee and I also have never discussed our conversation with Lander about the situation, not one time. The only topic we discussed regarding the entire situation has been her mentioning the newly installed furnaces in the home prior to the fire.

Arlee, Maria, and I still spend a lot of time together because Lander continues to work a lot. In addition to his job, Lander and Papa are building another triplex that Lander and I will use for income property. We all still visit Big Ma and Papa at the family house. The love from our foundational home still penetrates every one of us. It is still our family's private paradise and a place we come to just take deep breaths, relax, and recharge ourselves for whatever is in store for us the next week.

Maria has met a nice young man through Lander. He's a porter for the railroad. Daddy doesn't see him at work; he is in an entirely different area. Ruthie and Thomas are quite the pair. We laugh because when we see them, if there is any time that Ruthie's temper flares up, Thomas is like a bucket of water, pouring over a fire, and puts it out. They are total opposites, yet they are very close. Ruthie works at the Community Center now. She started out as an assistant to the visitors. Now, she is the part-time administrative assistant of the center, after taking some clerical and business classes at the business school in the next county. The director told Ruthie that after she graduates from school in nine months, it will become a full-time administrative assistant position. Ruthie will have her own office, if she takes the job.

Working full time requires additional work, with the upkeep of all the clerical files, financial accounting, and business meetings with many representatives of the community. What a long way my little sister has come—from Ruthie having a fight in a store, to sixteen hours spent in an adult jail cell. Ruthie had the profound realization of how unjustly and swift our freedom can be taken away from us and our lives put in the hands of strangers who are unmerciful.

We are all grateful for where the Creator has placed us, despite the scorn, hatred, and discrimination we go through every day. It makes us stronger, more determined to conquer and change things so our children will not have to go through this burden we carry. We appreciate each other and the times we have together, especially at Papa and Big Ma's.

We were all at the house one evening, when Papa started a fire in the pit on the grounds. Oh, we knew we were in for some good cooking when he started the fire. Usually, we can be sure that we will have chicken, fish, and corn on the cob, among other goodies. Big Ma had a strawberry cobbler in the oven; it was halfway done, and the aroma was flowing in and out of the house. Joseph and Thomas were at the end of the porch, playing with brand-new dominoes that Wilford bought to keep at the family house. Esther was in Baby Girl's lap as Baby Girl read her a book. Everything was wonderful—another Friday night all together, at the end of a hard workweek.

Wilford and Lander would be here soon. They usually work at completing the new triplex until five in the evening. The triplex is almost completed. Lander said we should get tenants in three months or so.

By 6:30 p.m. on Fridays, those two brothers have gone home, cleaned up, and are sitting at Big Ma's kitchen table, eating like they haven't eaten all week. If we all had our ways, we would stay out here all the time; it is like heaven here.

Maria, Arlee, Mama, and Auntie are in the bedroom with me and Big Ma. I haven't been feeling too good lately, and I haven't had my visitor in two months. I am almost certain that I am pregnant again. When I told Lander, he was so happy and immediately hugged and kissed me and told me I have made him the happiest man alive. Lander said to me at that moment that his life in the past was very sad and full of hurt, but ever since we met, his life has been changing for the better. When he said that to me, I hugged him and said that I hoped this baby would be a boy. As we were still hugging, Lander told me that it did not matter, boy or girl. We would love this new baby as much as we loved Esther.

I was very quiet, sitting on one of the beds at the family house.

"What's wrong with you, Peaches?" Arlee said, looking over her glasses with curiosity in her eyes. Mama and Big Ma already knew what was going on with me, but they did not say a word.

I looked at everyone and said, "I am very sure, but the doctor has not confirmed it yet; I think I am with child again." I could hardly get the words out my mouth when they all started hollering and ran over to hug me and each other. So happy, they were jumping up and down at the news.

"Oh, I know the baby is a boy," Baby Girl said with the biggest grin you have ever seen. "It's time for a boy. Yes, we really need this boy in this family."

By this time, Papa stood in the bedroom door, saying, "Everything okay in here?" He looked to Big Ma for an answer. "We hear all this screaming; we don't know if a gator is in here or not! What's going on with all this racket?" Papa continued to look perplexed.

"Everything is fine, dear. Actually, everything is wonderful! Peaches and Lander are blessing us with another great-grandchild!"

"What? Well, that is wonderful news. How are you feeling, Peaches?" Papa said.

After reassuring everyone that I am fine, it is nothing but joy and happiness.

I realized that Lander and Wilford were later than usual. I started feeling like something was wrong; then, I thought it must be my pregnancy hormones that had my mind thinking negatively. The ladies and I got on the topic of the new baby coming and that it is good that Esther and her new sibling will be close in age.

Suddenly, Daddy was standing at the bedroom door, calling my name. The first thing I thought was, *What is Daddy doing here? He is usually resting at home on his first night off for the weekend.* Mama, Big Ma, and I walked to Daddy, and we all reached him at the same time. "What's wrong, Daddy?" I asked him, grabbing his hand.

"Lander and Wilford ran into some problems at the triplex worksite. They are out in my car. Sheriff said it isn't safe to take them to the hospital right now. Peaches, Papa and the guys are with them. Wilford has some minor wounds, but Lander—they beat Lander up really bad. Peaches, he won't wake up either."

Before Daddy could say anything else, I ran by him and down the porch steps, calling Lander's name. When I got near the car, Joseph, Thomas, and Papa were carrying Lander; he could not even walk. I looked at his face; I looked for his eyes. *I just need to look in his eyes; then, I will know how he is. I cannot see his eyes! Where are his eyes?*

Lander's head and face were battered so badly that he was unrecognizable. I heard Big Ma yell, "Follow me; bring him here. Lay him on the bed!"

Lander's shirt was torn, his hands were swollen like clubs, his shoes and socks were gone, and his feet were bleeding. Daddy was right; he wasn't saying a word. He was unconscious.

"Lander! Lander! Lander, oh baby, who did this to you? Lander?" I was saying this to him as I followed the men who were carrying him into the bedroom. As they lay Lander on the bed, I saw the magnitude of his injuries—and the blood. *Why is it so much blood?*

I cried out to God, "Oh God, our Creator, please help us. God, have mercy on us. Touch his body, Master. Touch his body. You are the only one who can help us, God. In the name of Jesus." I felt like I went into a tunnel, watching all the movement and hearing Big Ma giving instructions.

With a calm yet firm voice, Big Ma said, "Get water in all the basins; bring the towels and linens. Ruthie, take the men to the chest full of the medicine jars and have them bring the entire chest in here and sit it over there."

Struck Down but Not Defeated

"Everyone, pray! Our Creator is right here with us. The Maker of heaven and earth is here, in all His power. Our God is guiding us with every step and decision we make right now. We are all God's vessels, and tonight, we will see the power of God in this place because He has told us and showed us all things are possible. Everyone must leave now, except Peaches, my two daughters, and Arlee. Baby Girl, little Esther is in your care until further notice. Ruthie and Maria, the care of this home and all those on this property outside this room are in your care until Lander is better. The two of can you start by cleaning up Wilford. Take care of his wounds, give him food for nourishment, and give him some of Aunt Candy's corn liquor out of the cupboard to calm his nerves." Big Ma looked at Papa, smiled, and said, "My love, our grandson needs to hear from his Creator while we are working on him. Can you get your flute, please?"

Papa nodded his head and went immediately to get his instrument.

Big Ma then said, "You men take Papa's responsibilities outside this room until God releases him from playing. Let Peaches know if the sheriff arrives. Everyone else, leave now. Pray, believe God, and continue to send all your love into this room. Remember, all is well, because God is faithful."

Somehow, hearing Big Ma composed enough to give everyone instructions pulled me together. What would I do if it were anyone else and not my husband? God tells me in His Word that when I am the weakest, that's when He steps in and becomes the strongest. I rely totally on God, my Creator, because He fights my battles. So let me do what I always do in times of emergency, and that is to work with these ladies to help someone in need.

I realized that one of the first things Big Ma does when caring for the sick had not been done, because her work on Lander's body was imperative. One of the first things done, when attending to one who is ill, if possible, is to set the atmosphere correctly. The atmosphere must be one that will promote healing—physically, mentally, and spiritually. God gives us everything we need for healing naturally through His earthly plants. I reached into Big Ma's chest that the men brought up and pulled out the jars of sage, sweetgrass, and red cedar. By lightly burning these natural plants in separate bowels, Lander would have additionally healing forces, created by God, working on his behalf.

We will get my wonderful man, who is lying in this bed, completely cared for, comfortable, and pain-free. Lander requires much care currently, and these ladies need my help more than ever. I will do what is needed of me now, as a caregiver. I must put away my "wife hat" and put it back on later, when we are through with his care. All Lander must do is rest and heal. I know God's healing power is at work within Lander, and it won't be long before he is alert and stable.

Big Ma saw me doing what needed to be done to change the atmosphere. She smiled at me and then winked her eye. Papa came into the room as I was putting the jars of plants back in the chest. He gave me a slight smile also and a look I had seen so many times before when I was growing up. It was a look of love, support, and courage. Papa brought a chair in with him, He put the chair in the far corner of the bedroom. Papa sat down in the chair and began to play his flute softly.

It took many hours to get Lander cleaned up, sewn up, in a fresh bed gown, and pain-free. Big Ma used the flowering plant yarrow to stop most of the bleeding for his outside wounds. We pray that he does not have internal bleeding, although Big Ma saw no indications. The town doctor will come tomorrow morning, but I trust Big Ma more than him. Big Ma gave Lander an antibiotic medicine for pain, so now we just wait for him to wake up, which he will do.

It was early in the morning, around two o'clock, when we were through. I left long enough to check on Esther, who was asleep in the bed with Baby Girl. Papa had brought me a comfortable chair from his office and set it by Lander's bedside. Mama, Auntie, Big Ma, and Arlee all refused to leave the room. They turned a sofa into a bed for Big Ma, and the others each made themselves a pallet on the floor.

Maria would come in every hour or so to check on her brother, talk to him, see if I needed anything, and to encourage me. Aunt Candy had arrived earlier, sometime after dark, with food, blocks of ice for Lander's swelling, and more soft cloths for the aloe vera and yucca balm bandages—these will help all the open wounds to heal faster.

I don't know all that Aunt Candy brought, but it sounded like it took a while for them to unload her vehicle. Mama said Aunt Candy was going to be here for a while because she brought many jugs of her corn liquor with her. Papa stop playing the flute a little before 3:00 a.m. Mama and Auntie made him go to bed to get much needed rest.

After Big Ma dozed off on the sofa, Auntie and Arlee lay down on their pallets. Mama sat in a chair at the foot of Lander's bed. She and Auntie were taking turns being on watch for Lander. I continued to sit by Lander's side, where there was the aroma of the fresh lavender I had put near his head. Both of Lander's hands were balm-wrapped, but I still managed to get my hand around his wrist, under the covers. I wanted to make sure he felt my touch constantly. I continued to whisper in his ear, telling him that I loved him and that I and the entire family were right here with him.

"We won't leave you alone, not for one minute," I told him. "I want you to get the rest you need but don't stay asleep too long because Esther, the new baby, and I need you very much." I talked to him just like we talk at home, just like everything was fine, because I knew that he would wake up soon.

I don't know when I dozed off, but when I woke up, Big Ma and Mama were cleaning dried blood from around Lander's eyes and then putting fresh ice packs back on his eyes, his face, and his lips. I still want to see my husband's eyes, the ones I looked so deeply into when we sat and talked for the first time on that wonderful day at the picnic. I felt myself getting emotional and quickly I pulled myself together. *I must be strong! I am better than this. Lander deserves a wife who can go through the fire with him, and that is what I am going to do.*

The men were back at the house early, helping with whatever was needed. Thomas was in the kitchen, helping Ruthie cook breakfast for everyone. Some of Lander's work buddies and other friends showed up also. I looked out the bedroom window and saw all the men on the side of the house, talking to Wilford and Papa, and I intuitively knew that they were discussing what had happened to Lander.

I know that there will be some type of retaliation from these men regarding what has happened. I can tell by the way they are huddled and all their body movements. Lander is the one who always calms the men down and makes them think before they act. I am not worried that they will be reckless in their retaliation, but I do know there will be retaliation, equal to what has been done—and at a time when those who did this to Lander least expect it. I got a cold chill as I pulled away from the window because I was letting my mind go to thoughts of who did this to my husband and why.

I went back to the side of the bed and whispered in his ear that I believe we have a baby boy in the oven and that his name will be Lander Banks Jr. My heart was broken as I looked at his battered, swollen face and body. Before I knew it, tears were running down my face, and I gently lay my head on his shoulder for a few moments. I couldn't lay my head on his chest like I do at home because of his injured ribs.

The doctor arrived from town early. He examined Lander thoroughly and was impressed with the care and treatment he had received. He did not feel that Lander had any internal injuries, other than possible bruising—no broken limbs—but the doctor felt he had fractured ribs, and his nose was broken. "My greatest concern for Lander are his head injuries," the doctor said. "Because of the swelling of Lander's face and eyes, I can't tell how badly his nose is broken or how serious the injuries are to his eyes. I have great concern about possible brain injury since Lander clearly had many blows to his head. If Lander does not wake up within twenty-four hours, we should consider having him hospitalized. I encourage you all to talk as much as you can to Lander, to try wake him up."

I was not encouraged by the doctor's visit and was glad to see him leave. I know it isn't the doctor's fault that he can't really help Lander, but I just know Lander will do much better right here at the family house, under the care of Big Ma, Mama, and all the other women in the family. I sat by Lander's side all day. Maria would relieve me for a few minutes to see the baby, but this is where I will be because I want to be here when he wakes up.

I could see Lander's swelling begin to go down, with all the continuous icing and medicated wrapping on his body. I asked Big Ma what she thought of each person coming in to talk to Lander. I wanted to use every stimulation possible, as the doctor suggested, to help Lander to wake up. Big Ma and Mama thought that it was an excellent idea. Mama suggested we have the visits in intervals, so it would not tire him out all at once. Big Ma and Mama had Papa play his flute often in Lander's room because it was a big part of his healing through Lander's ear gate. Papa also played music while Lander had visitors, hoping that it might remind him of all the good times we have had on the porch.

Papa put a chair on the other side of the bed for each person to sit in while talking to Lander, and I would remain in my chair on the opposite side. Papa sat in his chair, playing the flute, as, one by one, each person came in to visit with Lander, speaking nothing but positive encouragement. Some prayed with him, some spoke of the good times, and some tried to make the conversation as normal as possible

I would use Esther's baby spoon to put droplets of water in between those swollen lips to keep him hydrated. It took well into the evening for everyone to spend time with Lander. We gave Lander a lot of breaks so he would not get worn out.

Maria came in with Esther in her arms and sat in the chair next to her brother. Maria began to speak to Lander about when they were children and about their mom. Maria told Lander how much she is looking forward to having children of her own so they can play with Esther and the new baby coming. Maria began to cry as she told Lander he had to get better because she'd lost her mother, and she could not make it if something happened to him. Maria reminded Lander that at our wedding, Lander told her it was a new beginning for their family, no more sadness, and that we are all united. Maria then looked at me, while getting up from the chair with Esther in her arms, and said, "I am getting too upset Peaches, this may not be good for Lander, and began to walk away.

Arlee was comforting Maria when Lander moved his head and his legs and mumbled something. Aunt Candy jumped up off the sofa and said, "He's saying something! He's saying something!"

I got close to Lander. He turned his head toward me as if he could see me and said, "Move door."

"Move door?" I asked.

Then, with a slightly stronger voice, Lander said, "Move door. Maria move door."

I heard that clearly but did not understand. "I don't understand what you are saying, Lander. Maria, move door?"

Even though I could not see his eyes from the swelling, Lander seemed to adjust his head on the pillow so he could focus on me better. He said—in still a weak voice, but it was understandable—"Peaches, Maria move next door. Move next door."

Then I realized he was talking to Maria. He'd heard what she was saying, and he wanted her to move next door to us in the empty apartment. I repeated it to Lander and asked if that was what he'd said. And Lander nodded his head! *Oh, thank you, God! He is back! My husband is back!*

"Maria, go talk to him," I said, "He is talking to you. Talk to him!"

Maria went to Lander's side, crying. "Yes, brother, we need you. You want me to move into the apartment next to you?"

Lander had turned his head to the other side, where Maria was, nodded to her too. I came back around and kissed his puffed-up face and told him, "Everything is all right; God has healed you." He nodded his head again.

Aunt Candy had run out the room shouting, "He's talking, y'all! Lander is talking!" Everyone was so excited, and, one by one, they each came back in the room just to greet him and then left.

I know we have a long road ahead of us, but that does not matter to me. My husband is back among us, talking and responding. We are going to give him little doses of life, slowly and gently, just like Papa and Big Ma did for me, Ruthie, and Baby Girl when we were little girls. Lander has always been the protector for everyone. Things are different now; he will also be the protected one. Lander has been through the storm of his life, and he is coming out of it, healed and victorious. And God gets all the glory!

It has been two weeks since the horrible attack on our greatly loved Lander. My family and I are so grateful to God for the grace and mercy He has shown us. Lander is still recovering, and we are thankful for that. He has come a long way in just two weeks, but Lander still needs great progress before he can go back to his normal life. Lander is talking, sitting up in bed, and sitting on the side of the bed for short periods of time. Lander can eat some soft foods and is staying hydrated. This week, we will get him out bed completely to start walking, a little at a time. I believe that by the end of this week, Lander will be able to walk to the porch so he can sit and enjoy the fresh air.

The doctor from town has come out to visit Lander every three or four days and is incredibly happy with Lander's progress. The swelling in his face has gone down tremendously, although we still must continue with ice on his face every three hours. The swelling around his eyes is much better, but his eyes are still not completely open. His spirit is strong and relying on our Creator. Lander talks to Him like he has always done, but this attack has brought both of us much closer to our Creator in so many areas.

There are many things about the night of the attack that Lander does not remember, and Wilford is happy about that. Wilford is not the same; his injuries are more to his heart, mind, and spirit, something we are not as skilled in repairing. For me and all the other ladies, our focus has been following God's direction about Lander's total care and rehabilitation. In addition to Lander's care, everyone is trying to help each other to grasp what happened and how to get through it all. Being honest and talking about their feelings is helping everyone.

My elders have kept things from me intentionally. They want me to continue to trust them to handle things and only focus on Lander and our little family. They feel with me expecting the new baby, it is best that they take care of certain things until I get further along. I do not have any problem with that; they have always done what is best for me since I can remember, and I trust them. My family is handling the legal side of what happened that night to Lander and Wilford. The family told me when the developments that they are waiting for manifest, they will share everything with me. At this time, my elders have said that all that can be done has been completed, and soon, we will be able to discuss things.

When all the correct information is in, my elders will inform me so that I can make whatever decisions need to be made to achieve justice for Lander and Wilford. I can tell that things are happening by arrivals at the family house, followed by discussions that take place at the large table on the other end of the porch. The second day that Lander was stable, my grandparents, Aunt Candy, Wilford, and Maria rode into town to see Papa's attorney. They were gone half the day, so that must have been some meeting.

Sometimes, I look out Lander's bedroom window and see Papa carrying baby Esther. When Papa is walking around with baby Esther in his arms, he is most likely talking to her about trusting God, informing her about her ancestors, and how to have honest, hard work. Papa is telling my baby girl to save her money and that following the principles that he teaches will make her successful, and she and her family will have a wonderful life, without any persecution or injustice from some folks.

I know this is what Papa is telling my baby because this is what he has taught me, my sisters, and all the young folks in our family. He knows that my generation and beyond will be the ones to not live with prejudice and injustice. He has seen so much and been through so much in his life. Papa is my greatest inspiration in life; he is always there. He and Big Ma hold everything down through all the storms this family goes through. Papa always says we are his everything; that he was all alone in life, and then God gave him a family again—his family. I know Papa is trusting God through this, and I know Papa will never give up hope for what he wants for our family.

Having the love and support of my family and their trust in our Creator has given me strength and determination—whatever happens in my life, I will get through it. Papa says he is going to build another house on the land, the mini family house—that's what he told Big Ma we will call it. Big Ma says that our family is growing so we will need the room when the family needs to come for extended periods of time. I like the idea.

Aunt Candy is trying to have Papa build a juke joint on the

land too, but, of course, my grandparents won't hear of it. Aunt Candy has been such a help, and her contagious laughter is medicine for everyone. Her corn liquor has helped some of the family too; I must say. The corn liquor helps calm some of the family and prevents them from taking matters into their own hands when it comes to the attack on Wilford and Lander.

When Ruthie comes home from work, she and Aunt Candy cook dinner; they've done that ever since Lander has been ill. Thomas usually come two or three times a week to visit Ruthie and join us for dinner. After dinner, the three of them always sit at the table on the other end of the front porch, sip moderately on Aunt Candy's homemade drink, talk, and laugh until the sun sets.

Maria has been consistent in helping her brother and me and is spending more time with Esther. She and John, who is one of Lander's work friends, have been talking a lot, and he has been visiting her and Lander at the family house. Maria is starting to care for John.

Arlee knows of John through one of the girls at nursing school with her. Arlee says there has been talk that, in the past, John was known as a heart-breaker. The family has not seen any indication that this is true, but we have our eyes on him, just in case. If he doesn't show signs that he will hurt sweet Maria, the family has no problem with him. If John ever steps out of line regarding his relationship with Maria, that is an entirely different topic. The men have already had their "man talk" with John and have made sure he is aware of what's acceptable and what is not acceptable.

Our Reality

My parents and grandparents had the talk with me regarding the attack on Lander and Wilford. It was almost a month since the incident. I thought I was prepared for what they were going to tell me, but I don't think I could ever have been prepared for what they said. This is what my Papa told me:

"The men who attacked Lander and Wilford are men who were paid to hurt them. The men who paid for the attack are men who cannot be easily held accountable for their actions and for the payment given to the attackers. It is difficult for these men to be held accountable because they are very prominent and well-known government employees. One is in law enforcement. Everyone knows who they are and what they stand for, and they do not try to hide it. The men who paid for the attack on Lander and Wilford belong to an organization that hates people of color. The men who attacked Wilford and Lander have known of them since they were young and in school. These attackers have spoken to both Lander and Wilford in the past. One of the attackers is a second cousin to Lander and his siblings, on his mother's side of the family." Papa held his head down in silence.

I sat there for minute and remembered that Lander did tell me that his mother's family disowned her when she married Lander's father, a colored man. Lander had been very hurt about the situation. The pain he experienced was magnified when, years ago, Lander went to his mother's family and informed them that she was terminally ill. Lander felt that their knowledge of his mother's health condition would cause a change within his mother's family and somehow initiate a reconciliation.

This information did not have any effect on Lander's family on his mother's side. They reiterated to Lander that his mother had not belonged to the family for many years and had not been missed at all. Lander was told that he and his siblings were not welcome and that they were never to contact the family again. Lander never contacted them again. I was sorry that Lander, Wilford, and Maria had experienced such rejection and cruelty.

Papa continued with the information the family had for me. "Regarding these individuals who are the source of the attack, it is not the first time they have threatened Lander since his visit to his mother's family. These people kept up with Lander and his siblings over the years. They are aware that he has delivered United States mail, are familiar with his construction skills and projects, and know of all his investments within the city and beyond. These people have told Lander that he should stay in his place, and if he did not, he would pay."

I asked Papa, "What do they mean, 'stay in his place'? They asked Lander to stay away from them; he has, so what are they talking about?"

Papa explained, "There is an uncle and another cousin, a father and son, who have not been very successful in life, Peaches, even though they have good employment. Many people know that the family disowned Mrs. Banks. There has been talk that his mother's family feel that Lander's success, personally and in the community, is a slap in their family's face and, quite frankly, an embarrassment to them. First, the triplex you and Lander live in, and now with the new triplex almost completed, it is too much for them. Peaches, word is that they have stirred up other people about it too, and they want Lander to stop."

I could not believe what I was hearing. I thought the attackers had been strangers, men who thought they could take money or steal something at the worksite. This was far worse and so much more complicated. It is so hard to understand that the attackers are relatives who are jealous of their colored family members.

Papa tells me that our lawyer says we have three options. Option number one is that we can press charges, go to court, and possibly go to trial for assault to get justice, if the courts let it go that far. The second option is that we could sue them for financial retribution, meaning we try to make the court have them pay a large sum of money for what they did to Lander and Wilford.

When Papa did not say anything else, I looked at him and asked, "And the third option? Papa, what is the third option?"

At first, Papa said nothing; then he exhaled loudly and said, "The third choice, Peaches, is not do anything at all. You and Lander and all of us—just let it go. There are a lot of factors to consider if you decide on one of the first two choices."

My heart felt like it was going to fall out of my chest. It took some time just to soak it all in. I did not say anything for a while, and neither did my family. We all were sitting on the porch, fighting our feelings of defeat, with no words left to say. So many thoughts were going through my mind. It was as though the thoughts were coming in my head so fast and were all crammed in a space where there was not enough room for them. I felt like my head was going to burst.

I looked up at my people, my loved ones, my elders. They kept glancing at me, waiting for my response. I saw the fatigue on them. Big Ma had large bags under her eyes, and Papa was slumped in his chair like he sits when he has done yard work all day. Papa looked like he had the weight of the world on his shoulders.

Mama has been crying often since this happened. She thinks I don't know, but I know how her eyes look when she has been crying a lot. I know how she does her hair when she is just too tired to deal with it—one big braid, just pinned any kind of way on her head. When I looked at Auntie, she just gave me that smile she gives when she doesn't know what to say to me. I saw their exhaustion. They had been doing so much for weeks. I felt, at that moment, that it was time for me to pull myself together, get a clear head about everything, and get a direction for my family and our lives.

In a few weeks, Lander will be walking, and we will be able to go home. I don't know what I am going to do about all that I have learned tonight, but decisions do have to be made. To lighten the mood and give them some relief, I thanked everyone for all they had done, and I assured them that I would think and pray about what they had shared with me. I asked them not to worry and said that everything will work out, even though I did not feel that way at the time.

It would be another three weeks before Lander, Baby Girl, Esther, and I were back at home, trying to get our lives back to normal. Almost two months, but it is so worth all the time for Lander's recovery. He was walking, talking, eating, and able to take care of himself. He was moving slowly, but he was almost back to normal. Lander and I discussed the legal issues and the decisions many times at the family house and after we were back in our own home. Lander's father and Uncle Luke came from Ohio to help, visit, and give additional counsel, which Lander needed in so many ways. We were surrounded by all our elders, and that was wonderful for us.

When we did go back home, we were well equipped for whatever the future had for us. Papa and his workers, along with Wilford and friends, offered to finish the triplex for the rental properties. Lander accepted their offer to complete the building. Lander discussed with his boss about the possibility of working inside the post office to keep his visibility low. His boss was very kind and said that there would be a mail clerk position open in a few months, and he would see what he could do to secure that position for Lander. John, Maria's friend, also told Lander of several porter positions that were open with the railroad. Lander applied and within a week or so, Lander was hired for the porter job. It also would not start right away, so that gave Lander even more time to recuperate. We enjoyed our time off work together. We were getting excited about Esther's new brother or sister, and Baby Girl was such a help to me. Baby Girl never missed going to school and completed all her lessons.

With the wisdom we received from our family and the two of us discussing the issues about our legal matters, Lander and I agreed to leave the situation alone and try to put it behind us. We knew that a colored man, pressing charges against a noncolored person, would not move forward successfully. A legal case of that sort would only cause more confusion and possible additional threats and retaliation to us and our extended family. We did not want any trouble. We just wanted to mind our own business and live a peaceful life. With Lander working his two jobs on the inside, that would keep him for being seen by those who had issues with him. I prayed every day for God to protect us from harm and danger.

MH (Mental Health) A state of well being mentally, and all that it encompasses.

MHC (Mental Health Condition) A illness that affects an individual's thinking, feelings, mood, and behavior.

MHC Trigger: Colleen's father living with the pressure and anxiety of having to work in unsafe conditions when events have taken place.

MHC Trigger: The trauma of the attack on Wilford and Lander. The concern and the emotional stress of his recuperation.

MHC Trigger: The injustice of the law regarding the attack on Lander, with the pressure of knowing there will not be any pursuit of justice on Lander's behalf. Acceptance of the lack of protection for people of color.

MHC Trigger: The toll taken on family regarding not retaliating because of the attack. Having to plan life around no exposure to avoid confrontation.

MHC Trigger: Emotional trauma of elders seeing their children continue to go through what has been happening for hundreds of years.

Scriptural Support

For the Lord your God is He who goes with you, to fight for you against your enemies, to give you to save you. (Deuteronomy 20:4 NKJV)

What then shall we say to these things? If God be for us, who can be against us. (Romans 8:31 NKJV)

CHAPTER 8

Safely Engraved

L ander and I are doing well. It has been almost four years since the attack at the triplex. Many things have changed since then. We have our sweet Esther and two little boys— Lander Jr, who is three years old, and our baby boy, Norris Harolds Banks, who is two years old. We call the baby little Norie because Papa's first name is Norris and his last name is Harolds. Lander and I decided that whatever we had, boy or girl, we would name the baby after Papa. If it was a girl, we would name her Norrie Harlow Banks. Papa was so surprised and happy when we named the baby after him. Sometimes Papa and Big Ma walk around the land, carrying the boys, talking to them like they understand what they are saying.

We are keeping our word to each other about having many children, but I feel just one more will be enough for me. Lander does not care if we have ten children, but I see now, after having three children, that is very unrealistic. I realized before our marriage how much work caring for one child was. I just did not realize how much work was required to care for multiple children. Yes, one more will be enough—four children, may be another girl someday but not anytime soon.

I stay up late at night, working on the clothes that I sell at Mrs. Frances's shop. I do very well as far as sales go. I have a lot of repeat customers. They pass the word around, which always helps. I have sold some of my party dresses to customers as far away as New York and New Jersey. I now have new accounts in Ohio, Michigan, and Kentucky. Lander and I gave up on our dreams of having a dress shop. Selling my merchandise at Mrs. Frances's is our best way because we don't want to draw too much attention and cause trouble for our entire family.

Daddy and Mama still live in the end unit, and sweet Maria and John got married right after Lander Jr. was born, and now, they have two children—a girl named Janice and a boy named Lewis. All the little children make Esther feel like she is a big girl; she will be five years old on her next birthday.

Papa and Big Ma have not slowed down at all—still involved with keeping up the family house and land. Papa built the mini family house, as he calls it. It certainly is not little to me. As the family grew, the accommodations for everyone grew. Yes, our family is growing, and Arlee, Ruthie, and Baby Girl still have not had their children yet! Ruthie and Thomas are the next ones to get hitched. Ruthie told Thomas that if they were not engaged by the end of summer, she was through with him. Ruthie says she does not want to be too old to have children. They have planned a small fall wedding, for just family and close friends, at the family house. Thomas is still working for the railroad, as are Daddy and Lander.

The railroad is a good, steady job, even though the workers are asking for higher pay. Lander has met a lot of interesting and important people while serving them on the train. He has met people from all over the world and walks of life. Lander has favor with the clients he has on the train, and he listens to their advice on everything. Lander still works part-time as a mail clerk for the post office. He started taking part of that check to invest in the stock market, and soon, he says, we will be doing well.

The second triplex has been a financial blessing for us, but Lander finished renovations and made it into a duplex for us to move into. This way, we will have more rooms for our growing children and for Baby Girl to have her own room. Lander and Papa are going to add a big back porch, something like the front porch at the family house. We are looking forward to that so Lander and I can start making more family memories with our children and other members while sitting on our porch.

Before we knew it, it was Ruthie's wedding day. Our family was so excited and happy about this event. It is wonderful for all the family to be together again. We are not able to get together every weekend like we used to do. Thomas's family came from Alabama and Mississippi. They have visited many times, so we were looking forward to their arrival. I am happy for my sister; it is something she has wanted for a long time. For now, she and Thomas will stay at the mini family house, near Papa and Big Ma, while they make plans for their own home.

The wedding was everything Ruthie wanted. Lander and I stood up with Ruthie and Thomas and were their sponsors. Within a month, we had moved our things into the duplex, and it is very nice to have the extra rooms.

After a few months, we were finally settled in and comfortable. It was nice for Lander and me to have our own space as well. We haven't felt this relaxed and settled in a long time. I am glad that we made this move because Big Ma and Papa have been coming to visit a lot, and it is enjoyment for all. Lander, the children, and I go on Fridays to pick them up for the weekend, like they use to do for us when we were children.

It was one of those weekends when we had picked up Big Ma and Papa, and we were all feeling good about our weekend. Big Ma, Baby Girl, and Esther were planning on finishing jewelry they had been working on for a while. We were getting closer to home when we began to smell and then see smoke. Baby Girl kept saying it looked like it was coming from where our duplex was, and Esther kept telling her, no, it wasn't.

Much to our horror, as we got closer, we did see that it was our duplex, and it was engulfed in flames! Lander and Papa ran to side of the house to hook up the water hose. Someone in the area had contacted the firehouse because we could hear the screaming fire siren. Big Ma sat in the car, holding Lander Jr. and little Norie, and Esther sat in the back seat. Little Norie was fast asleep through all this chaos. Baby Girl and I were holding each other as we watched Lander, Papa, and neighbors try to put the flames out. Word had spread about what was happening, and before long, Ruthie, Thomas, Mama, and Daddy arrived.

Mama and Ruthie drove Big Ma and the children back to the family house so that the children would not see anything more of this incident. Women in the neighborhood were throwing buckets of water on the house, trying to help us. Some neighbors tried using water from their property to reach our home.

Where are the firemen? Why aren't they here to help us? I don't even hear the siren anymore. Despite all the efforts of Lander, Papa, and the other neighbors who tried to help, we could do nothing but watch our new home turn into a fiery inferno. The firemen arrived but in their old fire truck. They were able to put the fire out with the bigger hose, but by that time, it was much too late.

Engraved Secret Place

I looked at Lander; he was still trying to salvage what he could, going back and forth around the house. The firemen instructed Lander to keep away from the house for now because more burned wood was falling from all directions. Lander just stood there with his arms hanging to his sides and with despair all over his face. I walked over to him and put my arms around him, and tears began to stream down his face. My heart broke for him. He has worked so hard to give us a nice life. I kept telling him it didn't matter; as long as we have each other, that's all that matters to me. We could live in a cardboard box, and I would be happy with this man because he gives his heart and soul to all the people he loves.

Lander composed himself. Wilford showed up and tried to comfort his brother the best that he could. Thomas stayed with us; we just stood there, feeling numb from this horrible event. Papa, Lander, and Wilford walked toward what was the front of the duplex—thank God we did not have new tenants yet; it would have been a great loss for them too.

As Lander, Papa, and Wilford were walking toward the house, far away behind the house, we saw a cross—a cross that was starting to be covered with fire. Behind the cross we saw three men running from the field toward the road, going west. Lander, Wilford, and some of the men who were trying to help us took off running after the men. Papa ran behind Lander but suddenly stopped in front of the cross of fire. Papa stood there a minute or two and then fell to the ground.

I ran as fast as I could to get to Papa. "Papa! Papa!" When I reached him, he was lying on his side, and I could see him clearly because the field was lit up by the cross of fire. I sat on the ground and placed Papa's head on my lap. Lander and Wilford saw what had happened, turned back, and ran toward us.

Papa's eyes were closed. I cradled his head so he would be more comfortable and said, "Papa, you are going to be all right. You just need to rest, Papa. I'm going to take care of you. Don't worry, Papa. You are going to be OK."

Papa opened his eyes, looked into my eyes, and said, "Peaches, my grandbaby, Peaches."

By then, Lander and Wilford had reached us.

"Papa, we're going to get you to the hospital," Lander said. "I'm going to carry you, Papa. Trust me; I won't drop you." Lander was preparing to pick Papa up when Papa put his hand up for Lander to stop.

"Son, take Peaches and the family away from this place; it's not going to change." Papa took Lander's hand and looked him in his eyes. "Leave, son. Leave, and take Big Ma with you. Leave, Lander. Leave. They will not change, not here. Leave." Papa kept repeating those words—"Leave, leave"—while Lander carried him to the vehicle. I followed Lander as close as I could as he was rushing to get Papa some help.

As I was hurrying behind Lander and Papa, I heard a loud, sharp, crackling sound. I turned around and saw it was the burning cross making that sound. Something stirred inside of me; it was something I'd never felt before. Then, quickly, I thought about Papa and how he had collapsed in front of this cross. I started talking to him, spirit to spirit. *Please, Papa, fight like you taught us to fight. Papa, I love you! You can't leave us! Ruthie, Baby Girl, and I need you. Fight, Papa. Don't leave Big Ma, Papa.* I knew Papa could hear me. We are connected that way. I felt him; he was right here with me. *We need you, Papa. Please don't leave me!*

I continued to look at that horrifying burning cross and suddenly felt a great pain in my lower stomach. When I felt the pain, I knew it was the pain of my Creek clan and nation, the pain of my African family, the pain of Grandmother Golden Feather and all my ancestors who had to struggle, year after year, generation after generation. I felt the pain of my Papa, with all the years of love, demanding work, and devotion he put into his family so that our lives would be better. Now, my head was pounding like it was going to explode all over this field. I fell to my knees; I could hear all the words Papa told me over the years.

Papa wants us to live a life where we can be free to have homes, businesses, and prosperity without any threats, repercussions, and destruction from anyone. After all the time that has passed, after all Papa did, year after year, to make things better for his seed, things were still the same. He was crushed to see his grandchildren's home burned down to ashes, a home he was proud to help build with his own hands, a home full of love, where his great-grandchildren sleep. To watch the destruction of the home would have been enough, but on top of that, to see a cross burning on his grandchildren's backyard, knowing what it stood for, was just too much for my Papa to bear.

The pain in my stomach and head was so bad that I fell over from my knees, on the ground, lying on my left side. My heart literally ached when I remembered the profound hurt and agony in Papa's eyes as he gave Lander instructions to take us away from here. *Oh God, please help us. Son of David, have mercy on us.*

I heard a scream and another scream; it was a terrifying scream. The screaming got louder and louder! Then I realized— it was me screaming! It was me, and I was screaming for all my ancestors that had gone through so much and had to scream in silence because of the repercussions of those who heard their screaming. In the life they had to live, they could not let the hurt and frustration out, not by screaming or anything else, because it would be taken as negative action; if it were other folks, it would have been received with an abundance of compassion. I was pushed forcefully from deep within myself to scream for Papa and Big Ma. I bellowed for Ruthie and my sweet Arlee. I hollered and wailed for Grandmother Golden Feather and Grandfather Clarence. I shouted out for Auntie because of our experience of fear on the road that day to the family house and not knowing what the men would do.

I felt them all, even the family members we will never know about. I cried out in despair for them. For all my family that came before me, the ones whose names we don't even know, because they have been stolen from us, I bawled. I screamed for them all at the top of my lungs. I shrieked bitterly. I felt the weight and sorrow that my daddy's father felt as he lay next to his father, lifeless from the suffering and despair on that nasty slave ship. I howled like an animal because of the agony my great-grandfather endured, wondering what they had done to his beloved daughter when they captured them off their land in Africa and how desperate he was to help his family and get them back home to safety.

My people, my beautiful, blended people, suffer repeatedly and repeatedly. How long will this keep happening with no relief? We have not asked for a handout, just a fair chance, like everyone else. I could see Lander, beat up and bloody, all because he wanted to give our children the opportunity for a better life.

I don't know who it was, but someone was holding me tightly

as I heard myself screaming—screaming for all the times my people wanted to scream but could not. I start calling for my Papa, and he answered me. I could hear him, talking to me. I heard Papa; I could hear his flute.

"Papa, please don't leave me and Big Ma and the rest of our family," I said. "We have never been without you. Please, don't go. I know there is a season when you must leave, but not now. I am not ready; Big Ma isn't ready. Don't leave us, Papa. We need you. Papa, please don't leave. I'm scared to be here without you. I need you with me. Papa, please, please don't leave me."

I cried and cried so hard, like never in my life. I heard Papa's sweet flute starting to play. I felt the ecstasy there. I heard the noise of many waters, which is like the voice of God. I felt arms wrapping around me, but it wasn't Papa's big strong arms. The arms were small, like a petite woman. I knew instantly, in my spirit, that it was Papa's mama, Great-Grandmother Golden Feather, wrapping me in her love and care. Papa picked up me and Great-Grandmother Golden Feather and carried both of us someplace in his arms. Papa's arms were huge, much bigger than the arms that I have known all my life.

At that moment, Papa whispered, "I will be in the spirit from now on, Peaches. I cannot be with all of you physically on Turtle Island anymore. I have a heavenly body now, but I will always be with you—always."

My wonderful, strong, and caring Papa had transitioned to the place where I will go someday, and my heart ripped into many pieces. The pain I felt with the realization that Papa had passed on was unbearable for me. Papa knew this as he lay me and Great-Grandmother down. She was still holding me, warmly and safely. I felt huge waves of love and comfort. I was lying on the beautiful bright rug that was heavenly braided with love, joy, and understanding, like many years ago, when I was a girl. I was lying on the rug by myself now but still could feel the warm and safe presence of my great-grandmother. Papa covered me with the blanket of peace, with its glistening mixture of all the beautiful colors. He kissed me on the forehead and told me he loved me. Peace was penetrating all of me, to the core of my very existence.

I then experienced all that I had before, as a young girl, floating in the air in this wonderful place. The warmth of the sun on my body, the fragrance of the flowers, the birds singing in a heavenly way was all I knew. As I was floating in ecstasy, the sweet sound of Papa's flute and the noise of many waters was clearer to hear.

Then Papa whispered, "Forever you are engraved in His palm, young lady. Your name is chiseled in His palm. I am always going to be with you, in the spirit, in your heart, and in your mind. Be strong, Peaches. Don't be afraid. Our Creator will never leave you or forsake you. He will not leave or forsake all our family, from generation to generation, until the end of time. Peaches, never forget this: you are engraved in His palm."

Broken but Not Destroyed

There are only certain things I remember about that night. The crackling of the fiery cross, how it smelled, and how it lit up the field with light. I can feel Papa's head on my lap and me caressing his forehead. I remember seeing Lander running ahead of me in desperation, with Papa in his arms. I knew my Creator was right there with me. I am positive that he had Papa hold me all night. I could tell Great-Grandmother Golden Feather was with my Creator and Papa, and those three, all together as a team, were helping me and comforting me through the greatest heartbreak of my life. My Creator was rescuing me with His love in a way that He knew was best for me and what I could relate to—the greatest love of my life; my faithful, beloved Papa.

I woke up in a hospital bed. I felt restricted and saw that both my hands were tied to the sides of the bed. At first, I thought that I had jumped on someone and beat them up, like Ruthie did that day at the shop. Then I realized that it was not just my hands that were tied; my legs were strapped down too. *What's going on here?* I thought.

I didn't like being tied down like that and needed help, so I began to call for someone. "Hello, hello? Anyone here, please?" I called out loudly but not rudely.

A lady came in, wearing a nurse 's uniform. She smiled at me. "Hello, Mrs. Banks. I see you have awakened. How are you feeling?"

I thought about what she said and realized I had a headache and an awful ringing in my ears. Before I told her how I felt, I asked her, "Where am I? Why am I here? Would you please unstrap my arms and legs?"

The nurse responded kindly, "You are in the hospital, Mrs. Banks. You were not feeling well, so your family brought you to the hospital, and you were admitted on this floor. Would you like water or maybe juice?"

"Yes, I'd like water. Am I in the psychiatric ward?"

"Yes," she said. "Your husband, mother, and sister have been here in the waiting room for two days. Visiting hours are usually two hours a day, twice a day. Since you weren't awake, your family has been allowed stay until you were alert and stable. Would you like to see your husband? We only allow one visitor at a time."

"Yes, I would love to see him."

It was not long before Lander came into the room, and I was so happy to see him. He gave me a kiss on the forehead, put both my hands in his hands, as I said, "Hi, what happened? Why am I here? Where are the children?" I expected answers from him right a way so I'd know what was going on.

"Everything is all right, Peaches. You been through a lot, but you are OK."

As the nurse walked back in with my water, Lander asked her " Would you please take the hand and leg restraints off my wife now please"?

"I must get the doctor's orders to have the restraints removed," she responded in a sharp tone.

Lander said in a firm voice, "I am standing right here next to my wife. She is not going to do anything or go anywhere. Please remove the restraints now."

The nurse evidently could see that if she didn't do what Lander asked, she would have plenty of problems, so she heeded Lander's request.

It felt good to have the restraints removed, both my wrists and ankles were red and itchy from the tightness of the straps around them. The nurse left the room, and Lander and I were able to talk.

Lander took my hands again saying, "Peaches, I want you to understand that it might not look or feel like it, but everything is going to be all right. You hear me my love? I'm taking care of everything, and life will be good again. I will do anything so that you and the kids will continue to be happy. We must talk Baby. It's not going to be easy to hear, but you need to know something, Peaches. *First, I want you to know that the love we have is a special love, and with it, we can get through anything together, anything"*.

I saw the sadness in his eyes, that same deep hurt I'd seen on the first day we met. I knew what it was as silence fell in the room, as we looked at each other. The tears began to stream down Lander's face. I said to Lander, trying to make it easier for him, "Papa is gone, isn't he? Papa is with our Creator, his parents, and our ancestors. Is that what you want to tell me, Lander?"

Lander nodded, and we held each other and cried and cried. I knew that Lander was just as heartbroken as I was. He and Papa had become remarkably close and were like a father and son. Lander was closer to Papa than he had ever been to his own father. I heard everything Lander said to me, and I know he meant it when he said everything would be good again, I just could not see how.

It is difficult for me to imagine my life without Papa. I will have to take one day at a time. I will do the best that I can do, especially for Lander, the children, and Big Ma. I asked Lander how Big Ma was.

"She was crushed at first, but with everyone back at the family house and people visiting, she is getting stronger. Peaches, you had a nervous breakdown, and the doctor needs to get you stable. The medicine they gave you made you sleep for two days. The restraints were so you didn't hurt yourself; otherwise, I never would have allowed it. You'll need to take medication to help you stay calm and have a better outlook on life."

I did not like that idea and told Lander, "I'm not crazy."

Lander looked at me. "Crazy? Where did that come from? Peaches, taking medicine to help you means you are being smart and using the wisdom God has given the doctors to help us. This is a sickness, just like if we had a cold or tumor. We would want to do whatever the doctor is trained to tell us to do, wouldn't we? This is no different, Peaches, and I would prefer you never use that word *crazy* again, OK? You are an intelligent, kind, and beautiful woman, who happens to have a warm and caring heart. This life is confusing, chaotic, and cold-blooded most of the time. If we need help getting through these tough times and afterward, that's what we will do. That's why we will always have the finances to go to the doctor and get the medical help we need, for whatever part of the body that we need help in. We will critique the mental health condition medicine they give you, like we do the physical health condition medicine. If the medicine is not right for you, we will find the one that is and use it. If there ever comes a time that I need medicine or treatment for a mental health condition, I am willing and ready."

Lander helped me understand the truth about mental health, and mental health conditions, and it made intellectual sense. I never heard of anyone having that perspective toward mental health and mental health conditions. My knowledge of mental health conditions was only of the shame, guilt, secrecy, and stigma that is attached to it.

Lander said, "When my mother became ill and found out it was terminal, she went through a tough time. Maria took her to the doctor, and he recommended that Mother take medication to help. I know it helped tremendously, and it made a difference in how she spent the last part of her life, for the better. I want the best for you, and that includes your emotions and your mental health. I won't allow you to miss out on the best medical care because of other people's ignorance and misinformation."

I felt much better after my husband talked to me about taking medication for my mental health condition, and possibly speaking with a mental health therapist, if I needed to. "I'll take my time because I am a very private person," I told him, "and it would not be an easy task for me to discuss personal information with a stranger."

"I agree with you," Lander said. "We will take one step at a time, and one day at a time, and that is using wisdom."

Lander and I had a nice visit. We discussed everything, and I appreciated that—no sweeping things under the rug; let's discuss it, resolve what we can, and deal with what we can. Lander left and then Mama came in.

We hugged and cried some, but she was relieved that I was feeling better. I asked how she was doing with Papa's death, but she was not able to verbalize how hurt she was, especially with all the events that led up to Papa's transition.

"Knowing Papa's spirit is always with me is a comfort, but I will have to learn how to navigate my relationship with him in the spiritual realm. Our Creator is beginning to direct me in that area. Not seeing Papa alive in the physical realm will be an adjustment for all of us.

"How is Big Ma taking Papa's death" I asked.

"She is devasted but is constantly surrounded with lots of love, support, and care. Aunt Candy and Arlee are doing all the preparations for Papa's funeral and the arrangements for him to be laid to rest. Arlee and Aunt Candy will continue to get Big Ma's input on any major decisions, so everything will be just how she wishes it to be for Papa's homegoing. The family feels that's the best way for Big Ma right now, and it allows everyone else in the family to receive all the condolences, guests, and food that has been coming to the house in the past days."

Spiritually Connected Always

Lander gave Maria and Ruthie money to purchase my family the things we need since we lost everything in the fire.

Mama said many neighbors and friends have dropped off so many things we will need to start over again, new and like-new. It will take time to build everything up again. I have never felt that possessions are that important. I would allow a thousand houses and everything in them to burn to the ground to have Papa back. We can always replace possessions; there isn't anything on this earth that can ever replace the ones we love.

I am anxious to see my family, especially the children. Lander says that he and I will go back to the triplex where Daddy and Mama are. For the next few weeks, Baby Girl and Ruthie will focus mainly on the care of my children at the family house. My sisters caring for my children will give me time to grieve for Papa, rest, and refocus on my life. Big Ma will be happy with her great-grandchildren at her house and, hopefully, they will help to distract her from all the sorrow that she is experiencing currently.

Papa's funeral was hard to get through. Lander has only taken me to the family house one time since I came from the hospital and now, for the funeral. The medicine I am taking has me feeling much better, and I have been sleeping well.

At Papa's funeral, I was there and not there. For my mental health condition, my doctor gave me special medication for the day of the funeral. I did not view Papa's remains the evening before. I choose to remember Papa how he was when he was alive, not in a casket, sleeping in his earth suit. Papa was a good man, a wonderful businessman, and a friend to so many. His funeral reflected what type of man he was. I stayed in the car at the cemetery. I could not bear to see his casket lowered in the ground. I sat in the back seat of the car, looking at everyone at the gravesite. I could not help but cry as I looked at my family. I cannot imagine what we will do without Papa. Our family will never be the same without him.

I broke down and lay my head down in the back seat of the car. Suddenly, the door opened, and it was Big Ma, climbing in the back seat with me. She had me lay my head on her lap, like I used to do when I was a child.

"We will go on, Peaches; we will." Then she began to sing her and Papa's song.

> "Safe within, safe within, feels so good, safe within.
> Within Your palm, within Your palm, I'm engraved within Your palm.
> I'll conquer all, conquer all, not just me, yes, all my seed.
> Safe within, safe within, feels so good, safe within."

Big Ma kept on singing and singing. I kept crying and crying for my Papa. What hurt me so bad was for him to go like he did and with what he was in front of. He did not deserve that. He should have passed away at home, on his porch. He should have died with all his family surrounding him with love, like he did for his father. But for him to die under a burning cross, something he fought against all his life?

I just don't think I am going to make it; my mind is so crowded with all that Papa did to make things better for not only our family but all the folks in the community, especially the colored folks, because of their needs. Yet he died knowing nothing had changed. The ignorance and cruelty of people who dislike colored people killed my Papa, and nothing can bring him back. I was strong because Papa was strong, and he passed that on to me. Now he is gone, and I have no strength left. The evilness of people has hurt my Papa all the way to the grave.

I had not realized that we had left the cemetery and were at home in front of the triplex. Lander got me off Big Ma's lap. Big Ma kissed my cheek and said, "This will pass, Peaches. It will pass, baby." She started humming her and Papa's song over and over, as Lander and Daddy took me out of the car and into the house.

Ruthie, Arlee, and Maria were there in my bedroom, waiting for me. How did they get here before me? I just saw them standing at the gravesite when I was sitting in the car.

"Come on, sister; let's take those clothes off," Ruthie said as she sat me on the side of the bed and unbuttoned my suit. Looking at Ruthie just made me think of Papa more. All the wonderful times we had together over the years with Papa were running through my mind.

Ruthie put her hand under my chin to raise my head up. "You've always taken care of all of us all these years. Now it's time we take care of you. I love you, sis, and we are going to get through this together, OK?"

I just nodded my head. I was a wreck and could not pull myself together. I knew it, and it frustrated me immensely. Maria was taking my bun down, while Arlee took off my shoes. They had me in my sleeping clothes so fast I could not believe it. I followed all their orders and lay my head on the pillow, annoyed with myself because I could not stop crying. Head still on the pillow, I looked to the side of me, and all three—Maria, Ruthie, and Arlee—were lying in the big bed, crying with me.

Suddenly, Aunt Candy burst in the door with a shopping bag on her arm, talking with great concern, and loudly saying, "Hey, Peaches, how are you doing, girl?" Aunt Candy also had a big jar of her corn liquor with large straw in it.

Arlee jumped off the bed and yelled, "Mama! You know Peaches don't drink that stuff. Take it away, Mama! Now is not the time!"

Aunt Candy said, "Arlee, if you don't shut your mouth up and move out my way, I am going to knock your butt clear across the street. Now move your stuck-up booty out my way so I can give Peaches something that will really help her. And by the way, Arlee, you know Peaches is like my own baby but a lot easier to deal with than your difficult butt!"

Aunt Candy pushed Arlee out the way and sat down on the side of the bed next to me. She told me to sit up, and I did. Aunt Candy then said, "Drink this."

I started sipping on the straw.

Aunt Candy said, "This is for your sorrows and your mourning pain, Peaches. It'll help you, baby. You know your Big Ma and Papa use this at tough times too."

I was so out of it that I couldn't argue with anyone, especially Aunt Candy. Ruthie and Maria were sitting up on the bed now, on the other side of me.

Ruthie, looking surprised yet disappointed, blurted out, "You don't have none for us?"

Aunt Candy gave Ruthie a sly grin and said, "I thought you'd never ask." She bent down into her shopping bag and pulled out empty jars and a huge jug of her special drink. Aunt Candy filled Ruthie's jar, Maria's jar, and then her own.

I have to say—it was very tasty and also chilled nicely. Aunt Candy's drink had a nice little kick to it. "It's good!" I said to my aunt.

Aunt Candy replied with loud, contagious laughter. "Oh, wait until you feel the boost it will give you, Peaches; it feels much better than it tastes."

I had to admit I was starting to feel better. I had stopped crying, just a few sniffles here and there. "Arlee, are you going to have some with us?" I asked.

Aunt Candy answered before Arlee could respond. "Oh no, she doesn't want any, darling. It's not an imported wine from France!" Aunt Candy said this while speaking very proper and putting her nose up in the air deliberately.

"Mama!" Arlee screamed. That moment was so funny to me that I broke out into a laughter that I could not control. Ruthie, Aunt Candy, and Maria joined in with their laughter, laughter so hard that Ruthie was not looking and fell off the bed, drink and all. The way that Ruthie fell just boosted our laughter up one hundred levels for us all.

Arlee—frustrated with all of us because of our laughing and with Ruthie for spilling her drink on the floor—helped Ruthie up and picked up the jar off the floor, shouting, "It's not funny! This is not the time for this type of behavior."

Ruthie looked at Arlee and said, "Arlee, loosen up. If there was ever a time for this, it is now. What are we going to do? Let Peaches cry herself to death? You could use a little pick-me-up too. We all could."

Arlee looked at me. I smiled at her and raised my glass to her as if to say, *It's okay*. Before I knew it, Arlee had plopped in the bed with us, looked at Aunt Candy, smiled, and said, "Bring it on, Mama."

Aunt Candy smiled and handed Arlee her jar.

I looked at Aunt Candy and said, "What about the kids?"

"Between Baby Girl, your mama, Big Ma, and all the other visiting relatives and friends, your children will be taken care of and even get a little spoiled."

We all laughed again because everyone had let their hair buns down, changed from church clothes to lounging clothes, and were all about just being comfortable. Aunt Candy made sure we each ate a plate of food, including Lander and the guys.

Here we are again, us colored, blended, mixed, Negro, Muscogee (Creek) or whatever other name they're going to give in the future. As years go by, what people call us keeps changing. Yes, here we are, us girls, hanging on for dear life and, as usual, together.

I could feel Papa from time to time that evening and Great-Grandmother Golden Leaf, showing me that all these ladies are a part of them, and nothing can ever erase that fact. We laughed, cried, talked about everything, and ate a lot of food, plus dessert too. Aunt Candy had three jars of her special drink to our one, and it had not affected her at all. We didn't care about anything that afternoon and evening, nothing but that Papa was free and resting in peace now, and that Big Ma will always have a safe, happy life. We all guaranteed that.

I felt a little stronger now. Papa and Big Ma always said there is strength in the family unity; today proved that. We all ended up sleeping in the room together, as we have so many times over the years—in the bed and on the floor on pallets. We each went to sleep, knowing that for us, as women of color, this would not be the last time we will have to be anchors for each other. All these ladies, including Aunt Candy, are awesome and irreplaceable. Today, my sisters allowed God to use them, and they took a strong thread, made of love, patience, and laughter, and sewed my shattered heart back together, and for that, I will forever be grateful.

Big Ma said she and Lander wanted to talk to the family. It has been four weeks since we laid Papa to rest, yet it feels like just hours ago. I am adjusting to taking medication to help me deal with everything. It doesn't make me groggy anymore, and I have talked to a therapist once. Lander encourages me every day, and he says that what he is doing is nothing compared to what I have done for him since the day we met.

I feel even closer to Lander now, a deeper, more intimate closeness, where we have bared our souls to each other. We talked about Papa. My doctor told us that talking about our pain is a big part of the healing, processing the hurts, emotionally and mentally, in a positive way. Some days are better than others for me; the other day was a toughie.

I thought about Papa, how strong he was, and how, despite that all the people he loved so much had died, he pushed on every day until he met Big Ma, and then he rebuilt a new family. The family he built is our wonderful family, and oh, how I love everyone in it. I remembered that special day I had with Papa when I was still a girl.

That was the day that I asked Papa why he never gave up. That was the first time I had the sacred journey to the same secret place that I went to on the night Papa transitioned. What a wonderful place. Before I knew it, I was crying again as I walked to my bedroom chest and opened the top drawer. There, in the left-hand corner of the drawer, was my velvet-and-satin keepsake box that Big Ma made for me when I was so young.

Mama had told me to keep the note Papa left me in a safe place. I obeyed and still have it in the treasured keepsake box. I have only read it one other time, when Lander's mother died. I read it to get encouragement to pass on to Lander.

I sat on the side of the bed, took out my precious note from Papa, and began to read:

> To Peaches. The answer to your questions:
> How did I not give up? How did I keep going?
>
> Answer:
> God, our Creator, wants the island to listen.
> God, our Creator, wants the nations to listen.
> God, our Creator, will never leave you or give up on you and will never abandon you.
> Trust God, the Creator, with all your heart.
> Don't listen to your negative thoughts or other people's negative thoughts.
> God, our Creator, will guide your steps every day of your life because He will be a lamp to your feet, and He will be a light on any path you are on.
> God, our Creator, will not lie to you. He can't; He is not a man.
> With God, our Creator, all things are possible.
> God, our Creator, will strengthen you, and He will protect you from the evil one.
> Lastly, Peaches:
>
>> Can a woman forget her sucking child that she should not have compassion on the son of her womb? Yea, they may forget, yet I will not forget thee. Behold, I have engraved thee upon the

palms of my hands, thy walls are continually before me. (Isaiah 49:15–16 NIV)

I love you, Peaches.
Your Papa

I held my note from Papa against my chest as tightly as I could. I cried and said, "Thank you, God. Thank you for Your reminder through Papa's note. I will walk stronger now because You have equipped me for all things. I won't give up, ever. Papa trusted you, God, and so will I."

I will be the overcomer example for the family from now on. I can do all things in Christ. I will walk by faith and not by what I see and what I feel.

Papa's Orders

I knew this meeting was going to be something else, with all the family there, so hurt about Papa's death and everything involved in his death. The law has not helped us in bringing whoever burned our home down to justice. They also have not found who is responsible for the burning cross on our land. All this led to Papa's massive heart attack and took him away from us. Our family knows, though; yes, we know some of the law officials do not have to look any further than their own backyards to find the culprits. We are using the wisdom our Creator gives us to deal with the things we can't change, especially since it will only cause more heartache for our family. We all believe what God says about reaping what we sow. We know that God is going to take care of all the individuals and organizations for all they have done to our family.

Our Creator will take care of them better than we can because he knows everything there is to know about them, and He says that vengeance is His. Big Ma, Lander, and I have been talking about serious things for the last past two weeks. We have talked and cried and prayed many days and nights at the family house and at the triplex. Big Ma and Mama have had us spend more time worshiping God with our singing, even more so because God inhabits the praises of His people. Our family needs God's presence more than ever.

I do not know how the family will take our decisions, but a change must take place. Lander and Big Ma deciding to include me in their discussions and decisions means so much to me. When I had my breakdown, I thought that they would change toward me, feel differently about me, and not value my feelings or opinions. Both Lander and Big Ma said I should never feel that way, that the breakdown was just a manifestation of all the stress and heartache we had to deal with in life. They keep telling me that taking care of our emotions and good mental health is just as important as taking care of our physical health. Total wholeness is our goal, as Big Ma always said, but I never realized what she was talking about until I started recuperating from my breakdown.

Lander says that there would be many happier people on this earth if they realized and practiced these facts about their thoughts, minds, and emotions. I am learning, through the love, acceptance, and support that my family gives me, that I should have no shame about the breakdown or the mental health condition that I am experiencing. Shame and false guilt are things that can destroy a person, so I will not allow that to penetrate me. I'll have no part of that. I will share with everyone who God sends in my path, to help others find the freedom I now have.

We were all in the kitchen at the family house, some sitting at the dining table and others in extra chairs that were brought into the large kitchen. Big Ma started out with prayer and thanked our Creator for sharing Papa with us all those years. Everyone still cries instantly when Papa's name comes up or if someone starts to sit in his rocking chair on the porch but just can't. Papa's flute stays in the velvet pouch he always kept it in, on the little table between his and Big Ma's rocking chairs.

Big Ma had a lot to say, I could tell, because she was not too talkative prior to our going into the kitchen. Big Ma started out by telling us that she loved us, that Papa loved all of us very much, and that we were the most important thing in his life besides his Creator. We all knew that in our hearts. All he ever did was support us, nurture us, and help us to be the best we could be. Big Ma said that she and Papa had started to talk about things about two years ago that they had never talked about before.

Big Ma shared that we, as a people, have spent our lives trusting God and following His Word, which is good. She said, "Because of our social position in our county, we have had to learn to be experts with the habit of holding our peace in big and small circumstances. We are not able, even though we may want to, to express what we are feeling or even defend ourselves. Holding things in too much causes us to become toxic on the inside, which causes mental and physical stress on our bodies. To be able to face our feelings about our lives and all the challenges and to be able to talk to each other about our feelings is important to our overall health.

"Papa and I had frequent conversations about the fact that it doesn't make any difference about our financial security, how hard we work to get ahead, or who we know in positions to help us. We are unable to progress in any way. The fact remains that no matter what we do, we will never have equality. We will never be able to have the same as others or more, without paying a price for it. Our children will never get the education we want them to have or be in the environment that shows them they are as smart and capable as the next person. Generations have been working for this to happen, but it will not happen for us, not in the South.

"Papa and I realized this and want our children to have a better chance at a different future than what we have had. Papa and I thought things would change, but with the events of the past several years, things not only did *not* get better, but things have gotten worse. We live in an unsafe, toxic, and unhealthy environment. The piece of heaven we have on this land—we are free and happy, until the day someone feels we don't deserve what we worked for and built. Then they take it from us. When you leave this property, we want to know that you are safe and have a fair chance at life. Papa and I no longer believed that what we worked hard for all these years can be obtained in this state.

"For that reason, Peaches, the oldest of our grandchildren, and Lander are going to be moving away from here to a place that is conducive for the growth and development of the children in our family. This is what we want from generation after generation, until the end of life on this earth. We no longer will live in an environment that is destructive to the family, as individuals and as a unit.

"I want you to know that I will be moving away with Peaches and Lander. Papa and I had talked about this move, decided to do it, and began to make plans for it someday. Papa and I were going to talk to all of you about this over the Thanksgiving holiday. With Papa's passing and the fires, we have decided to speed up the plans and go ahead with the move as soon as possible. Also, we have not shared one thing with the family, and that is that one of the last things Papa said to Lander before he left us was for Lander to take me and the family away from this state. He wants us to have a fresh, new beginning, and because this is what Papa wants, it's what I want.

"Papa always did what is best for this family, and his wisdom will carry on with us, even though he is no longer with us physically but with us spiritually. For any of you who want to join us, we will work together for the one goal of a fresh start, for a better future for each of your families as a unit, and as a family group. Lander and Peaches, along with me, will help support your move financially and in any other area pertaining to the move. Take time to think about this opportunity, and feel free to ask us any questions, whenever you want."

So many of our family members were shocked, but it was

a pleasant shock to them. Big Ma turned the meeting over to Lander.

"There are many great opportunities, especially in Ohio," Lander said. "My father and Uncle Louis live in Ohio and have done very well there. Hudson, Ohio, is a place that I believe is the best place to live, after much research of the cities. Hudson, Ohio, is a city that is very fair with all people, including people of color."

Lander and Big Ma emphasized that the move would take courage and strength but would be worth it. The family would be meeting again soon, and Lander would be going to Ohio to prepare for everything.

After the blessing of the food, Ruthie and Thomas made the happy announcement that they are expecting a baby, which was the great boost of happiness our family needed. Ruthie will make a great mother.

Lander traveled to Ohio to prepare for our move and to seek future employment. While my husband was away, I helped Big Ma pack up the things that she wanted to take to Ohio and get rid of the things she no longer wanted. The hardest part for us, especially Big Ma, was packing Papa's belongings, which we decided to take to Ohio with us because we could not throw his things away. Papa's belongings were part of him, and we had to keep them and hold on to them as the treasure they are.

Lander and I did not have much to pack much because we lost everything in the fire, except for the new things we purchased and the donations people gave us right after the fire. After a month or so, everyone made their decisions. Baby Girl wanted to go with Lander and me, our children, and Big Ma. Arlee and Jacob also were going. Arlee is an LPN so she would not have a problem getting work at a hospital.

Lander had decided to become a trucker and work independently for companies. Jacob was also interested because it paid well. Maria and John and their three children also were moving to Ohio. Ruthie and Thomas were going to stay since the baby was coming; they would be staying in the family house because Big Ma did not have the heart to sell the property yet. Ruthie and Thomas did say that they planned to join us in Ohio for a new life by the time their baby is two or three. Aunt Candy will be moving into the mini family house by Papa and Big Ma's family house. Daddy was not ready to retire, so he and Mama would continue to stay in the triplex and would handle getting the rent from the other two apartments every month for us.

It was bittersweet leaving behind what we were so accustomed to. So many memories, and most of them were wonderful memories. The fact that Ruthie, Thomas, and Aunt Candy were going to still be there on the land made it a lot easier and not so final. The day before we left, movers came and loaded everything up and drove ahead to Ohio. Weeks before the drive to Ohio, Lander had purchased a new station wagon, with plenty of room for everyone.

Big Ma, Baby Girl, Arlee, my two babies, and I all rode in the back, and we still had plenty of room. Lander and Jacob sat up front, with Esther sitting between them. Esther switched up sometimes and sat with us girls when she thought she was missing out on the fun we were having with our car games.

Lander and Jacob did all the driving to Ohio. We had three picnic baskets full of food; Ruthie and Aunt Candy had been cooking the day before we left. We had enough food and drink to get us out of the South, for sure; then, when we got close to Ohio, Lander said it was safe to go to the restaurants on the way.

As we pulled out from the family house land, the memories flooded my mind. I started feeling a lump in my throat, and I heard Baby Girl sniffling. We looked at each other, and Baby Girl put her head on my shoulder.

I could see Papa, walking to meet us on the road the last time we walked there and how he wouldn't let us walk that road ever again. I could feel the relief from him taking Baby Girl off my back. I remembered Papa fishing all those days down by the falls and us girls helping him. I remembered all the family gatherings and heard the laughter of us girls acting silly. It's amazing how

I can smell Big Ma's fry bread and taste Papa's chilled sun tea. I thought about Lander and me—the first time he told me he loved me was right here at the family house—and I thought of our unforgettable wedding day.

"How blessed we are, Baby Girl, to have so many happy memories, right?" I said, trying to cheer her up. Baby Girl was so emotional that she could only nod her head as tears streamed down her face.

"Now we get to make new and wonderful memories in Ohio!" Big Ma said with forced cheer. She looked down at little Norrie as he was snuggled tight on her lap.

I looked up at the sky, and I thought of Papa. I thought of the many nights over the years, sitting on the porch under these stars, listening to him play the flute, and us singing Big Ma's song. I thought about what life would be like in Ohio, and a little fear came over me. I had taken Papa's note that was in my satin-and-velvet box before I packed it and had it in my pocket every day since then. I took Papa's note out of my pocket and held it in my hand as we drove down the road. I had a feeling I was going to have his note out a lot in our new life in Ohio.

Big Ma looked at me and smiled; then she said, "Who is going to sing with me?"

Before anyone could answer, Big Ma started singing loudly, "Safe within, safe within. Feels so good safe within. Within Your palm, within Your palm. I am safe within Your palm." We all started singing along with Big Ma. We sang her song for a while. We cried, laughed, and talked about all the days at the family house.

I felt the love of my Creator and His lamp to our feet and His light to our path. We were being directed by our God, and we would continue to follow His lead all of our lives. Our Creator was leading us to Ohio, where justice, blessings, and peace awaited us. I was excited about what was ahead for us and all our family. There was so much more to come! I felt Papa's presence, and I knew he was with us. We were safe and loved so much by God, our Creator—so much so that He engraved us in the palm of His hands.

MH (Mental Health) A state of well being mentally, and all that it encompasses.

MHC (Mental Health Condition) A illness that affects an individual's thinking, feelings, mood, and behavior.

MHC Trigger: Tragedy of Colleen and Lander's home destroyed by fire. The loss all of family possessions in the home.

MHC Trigger: Cross burning in the back of the property.

MHC Trigger: Papa's death.

MHC Trigger: Colleen's breakdown.

MHC Trigger: Papa's request for family to leave the South.

MHC Trigger Alert: Decision and road to new life.

Scriptural Support

> For I know the plans I have for you declares the Lord, plans to prosper you, and not to harm you, plans to give you hope and a future. (Jeremiah 29:11 NIV)

> For God has not given us the spirit of fear, but of power, and of love, and of a sound mind. (2 Timothy 1:7 NKJV)

Printed in the United States
By Bookmasters